PERCIPIENCE

A Cosmic Horror Novella

Michael Sellars

Copyright © 2024 Michael Sellars

All rights reserved

The characters and events portrayed in this book are fictitious. Any similarity to real persons, living or dead, is coincidental and not intended by the author.

No part of this book may be reproduced, or stored in a retrieval system, or transmitted in any form or by any means, electronic, mechanical, photocopying, recording, or otherwise, without express written permission of the publisher.

Cover art created by the author using public domain images from Unsplash by Joshua Earle and Danny Lines.

For Liam Colebrook. An absolute gent.

The Guests are scattered thro' the land
For the Eye altering alters all
The Senses roll themselves in fear
And the flat Earth becomes a Ball

    WILLIAM BLAKE, THE MENTAL TRAVELLER.

DAY MINUS ONE
COMPLEV 1

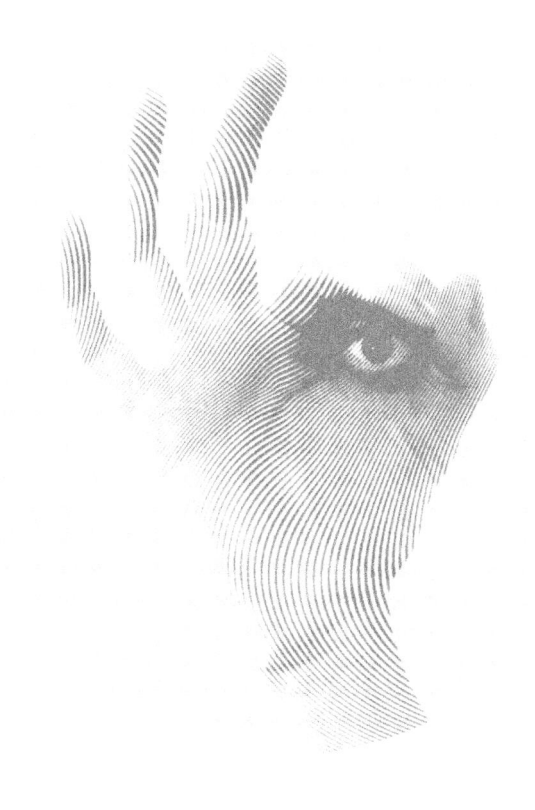

To: Carl Lyons
Subject: Whitecoats (Iteration 104)
Attached: WI104Profiles.docx

Morning Sir,
I've attached the write-ups of our four new whitecoats. I appreciate you're busy, so here's the in-a-nutshell overviews.

Andrew Keep. A forty-five-year-old financial disaster from Liverpool. His wife died last year leaving behind a heap of debt, which he's successfully managed to turn into a *mountain* of debt. We've stepped in 'just in time' to prevent his home from being repossessed and what's left of his dignity being fed to the dogs.

Cassandra Flint. A twenty-four-year-old classroom assistant from Birmingham. Pothead and what's-your-star-sign type. We're having a possession-with-intent-to-supply charge dropped in return for a spell at the Observatory.

Jagrav Panchal. A twenty-eight-year-old 'entrepreneur' from Hounslow. His parents think he used his BA in Business Management to create his own successful property management firm. It's the 'successful' bit that's misleading. He's in debt to some very unsavoury investors. And by 'investors' I mean gangsters.

Fiona Needles. Thirty-three years old. From Sheffield. An enochlophobia sufferer. Fear of crowds. Two suicide attempts. Last one very nearly successful. She sees our offer of a well-paid job away from the possibility of any crowds as a potential "new beginning".

The CCA tests produced low scores for all action-related criteria, with intellectual-curiosity readings all above average. These guys are definitely Watchers and Ruminators, not Doers. All have good-to-high literacy levels should we need their journals after-the-fact. It's all in the attachment. If you have any questions or concerns, just let me know.

Regards,
Ben Hopkirk
Project Administrator
Department of Incidents and Occurrences

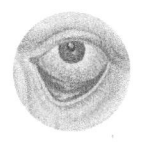

From the private journal of Ben Hopkirk:

First day in the new role went well. Didn't fuck up anyway. The whitecoats are all on-profile. It's been eye-opening seeing just how many flavours of failure there are. Just waiting for Lyons to give the nod, rubber stamp it or whatever he does and they'll ship out tomorrow. Lucky buggers. Three months of doing fuck-all as far as I can tell. Sweet. This is the weirdest place I've ever worked, and I've worked in some weird places. The whole department is geared toward opacity, inelegance and oblique-to-non-existent communication. It's as if they're working all-out to fail. Like failure's the goal. Maybe that's why they picked me – ha-ha.

Went to visit Dad. He looked at me like he knew me. Just for a couple of seconds or so. Maybe I imagined it, but it was nice. Really nice. Then he called me Brian and asked me if I'd stolen his toothbrush. Same old.

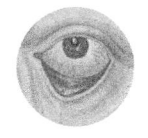

To: Ben Hopkirk
Subject: Re: Whitecoats (Iteration 104)

Approved.

Carl Lyons
Senior Project Manager
Department of Incidents and Occurrences

DAY ZERO
COMPLEV 1

From the DIO Journal of Andrew Keep:

Hi Sarah. How's it going? That lanky streak of piss in the shiny suit, Hopkirk, said nobody's going to be reading these journals. It's just for our mental health. Processing, decompressing or some such bollocks. So, I've made the executive decision to use mine to keep you posted on what's happening in the land of the just-about-living.

I don't know what qualities they think I have that make me an ideal candidate for the position of 'Non-Processing Analyst' (whatever *that* is) but they put me on a plane then a helicopter and hours later we're landing in a clearing in a forest. Trees as far as I can see. Big, fat deciduous trees and tall pines all mixed up together in a way that doesn't look quite right. Beautiful, no doubt, but not quite right. It's warm. A little humid but nothing like tropical. I wonder where we are?

And yes, you heard me, a *helicopter*. With blacked-out windows no less. I felt like Jason fucking Bourne. If Jason Bourne had a beer gut and greying hair and an expression of perpetual cluelessness. The whole time I'm sat there – the slapping of the rotor blades overhead too loud even with ear defenders – I'm wondering why the fuck have they picked me for this gig? I mean, I don't really know what 'this gig' is but given the fact that most of my work experience has been at the arse-end of retail since I left school with five O Levels and mediocre woodworking skills…

Blackford, the company guy who took us up to the Observatory, he's not as shiny as Hopkirk and lacks the gobshite aura. Older, too. About my age. Looks like he's been through the mill and needs a couple of whiskeys and a Heminevrin to get himself to sleep at night. Sound familiar? Anyway, he says it's going to be (and I'm quoting him here) "a fucking cinch. Nothing to it. Watch. Take notes. Learn nothing." Seriously, I'm not making that last bit up. "Learn nothing."

Christ, I used to be such a good sleeper. My head would hit the pillow and *poof* I'd be out for the count. I remember you saying to your friend, Katie, "Andy doesn't fall asleep, he *deactivates*. Sometimes, it's just a little bit creepy." One of the few things I was good at, sleeping. Sleeping, shooting pool and making you laugh.

I suppose I should introduce you to the other 'Non-Processing Analysts' (I mean, they *tried* to explain it to me, but…):

There's Jag, a young Indian lad. Keeping his powder dry that one, but he seems okay. Then there's Cassie. A bit of a hippy. Doesn't smell of weed but looks like she *should* smell of weed, you know? And Fiona. Fiona's one of those nervous types. As soon as you start speaking to her you instinctively lower your voice. She reminds me of your cousin, Imelda. Nice but skittish.

It's about a twenty-minute walk from where the helicopter lands, up a dirt track, and we're at the Observatory. There's no dome where a telescope might poke out, but that's what they call the place. The Observatory. It's just a big concrete hexagon. Three stories, small windows. Balconies on the first floor. There's a name for this kind of architecture, I think. Brutal? Something like that. You'd know the word. Walking dictionary, you are.

Inside everything's white. I mean white-white. So clean. Hospital clean. Doesn't smell like a hospital though. Thank fuck. Had enough of that smell to last me a lifetime. People who haven't spent much time in hospitals, in aseptic environments, have no idea just how much clean can stink.

Anyway, I'll give you the tour...

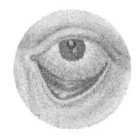

From the DIO Journal of Cassie Flint:

It's as horrible on the inside as it is on the outside. There are no vibes. None. It's clinical, soulless. It feels like I'm walking into a machine or a massive piece of medical equipment, an MRI or something. Feels like the whole place has been bleached, scrubbed and sluiced down until there's nothing natural left. Not one speck of life. Not the slightest fizz of energy.

The ground floor is just a big hexagonal space. There's the wall with the entrance door. There's the wall opposite, with a chrome and steel spiral staircase twisting up to the next floor. And then there are the four remaining walls. There's a door in each of those walls. Our names are on the doors. Andrew, Jagrav, Fiona, Cassandra. Not Cassie, Cassandra, like I'm in trouble. Again. It certainly feels like punishment. All this bleached-out nothingness. Not sure what that's going to do to me, and three months of it.

It's not the first time I start thinking I've made a mistake, that this whole thing is so *covert* it's got to be rotten. But then I think about the possibility of six months in prison, a fine I can't pay and the job I can't afford to lose. Then there's Mum. She would shit a brick if she found out I got a speeding ticket never mind doing hard time as Balsall Heath's answer to Pablo Escobar. She wouldn't be able to show her face at Wine Club on Thursdays, and they'd probably expel her from Saturday morning's Nordic Walking Club. Jesus, it's bad enough that I live in Balsall Heath. The shame! The shame!

So, yes, I think I've made a mistake coming here. But it would have been a bigger mistake to take the possession-with-intent charge.

On the plus side, my room has a whole shelf of old film noirs. *Vertigo*, *Laura*, *The Lost Weekend*, *Out of the Past*, *Ace in the Hole*, *Night of the Hunter*, *Spellbound*, *Pickup on South Street*... It's a fantastic selection. All VHS, though, and I have to watch them on a clunky old VCR and a TV that looks like it was put together by a cabinet maker. Took me about twenty minutes to get the thing working.

I don't remember mentioning that I like film noir in my interview. But I must have.

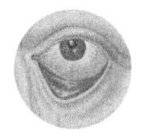

From the DIO Journal of Jagrav Panchal:

Fucking hell. Everything's white but me in this place. Shouldn't complain, though. It's all very modern. And the first floor's not bad. In the middle of this big, penthouse-style space, there's a compact living room area with leather sofas, a coffee table and even a vintage floor lamp that looks like it might be worth a bit. There's a kitchen area on the far side of the space, high-gloss units, marble worktops and all chrome accessories. Very nice. Like something you'd see in a style magazine, Wallpaper or one of those.

I might have room to think here, to work things out. My five-year plan. Something that doesn't involve a lengthy hospital stay and a permanent limp.

Fuck. What a mess. What a fucking mess.

But not anymore. Hopkirk said so. A three-month tour of duty at the Observatory and all debts are wiped out. Clean slate. Just not sure I trust him. There was something a little too *shiny* about him. I've met people like him before. You get a lot of them in the property investment game. Teflon types. Nothing sticks to them. The shit just slithers off and deluges some other poor fucker who just happens to be walking by at the time. Sometimes I'm the poor fucker. Sometimes I'm a bit Teflon myself. But it's not as if I have a whole suite of choices open to me right now, is it? It's this or plaster casts and morphine. And that's if I'm lucky. Khalid and his boys might want to do more than just splinter my kneecaps. Might want to use my skull for golf practice. Khalid loves his golf. And hurting people. Don't forget that. Khalid fucking *loves* hurting people. It's his jam. The psychotic bell-end.

Anyway. Fuck it. I'm here now.

Wherever here actually is. They didn't tell us. *Wouldn't* tell us. But the length of the flight tells me we're a long way from Hounslow. A long, long way from Hounslow.

Anyway.

There are four doors off the main space that lead out onto balconies. There's a sign on each door. 'Weather', 'Flora', 'Fauna' and 'Acoustics'. Next to each door, there's a big whiteboard with a grid on it divided into lots of smaller squares, marked 'Day 1' through to 'Day 90'. On the coffee table, there were four envelopes, one for each of us. In each one, there's a hardbacked A4 journal (I'm writing in mine now) and a 'task card'.

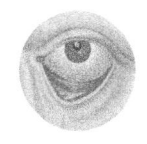

From the DIO Journal of Fiona Needles:

To be honest, this is a lot better than I expected. It's big and roomy, no clutter. And there are no people for (presumably) miles, just the other Non-Processing Analysts and they seem okay. Keeping themselves to themselves. No touchy-feely stuff. No personal questions. Probably that'll come later. I might be okay with it when it does, if I have enough time to clear my head, build up my defences. My 'task' will help with that. It's the simple, mechanical, just-get-on-with-it sort of work I can lose myself in. All our tasks are like that. Basic stuff.

Despite all that, I got a bit panicky (not breathless panicky but panicky enough) and asked Blackford the helicopter guy what happens if something goes wrong, if someone gets ill or something? What if someone gets appendicitis? What if someone has a heart attack? I mean, that Andy does not look in the best of health. What if someone – say me, for example – just freaks right out and can't take it anymore? I didn't ask him that. I was just thinking it. I'm always thinking it. He took us up to the second floor. It's much smaller, and there's nothing there but a chair, a desk and a really old-fashioned looking radio, like something you'd see in a black-and-white war film where they're sending messages back to Blighty in code.

"Just radio for help," he said. "But you won't need it. Just sleep, eat, relax and carry out your tasks.

There's nothing to it."

In my case, there's painting to keep me occupied too. In my room, there's a load of watercolour supplies. Good quality stuff, too. There's Windsor and Newton paints, Strathmore paper and Isabey Kolinsky brushes. With three months to kill, I might even get good at it. Don't get me wrong, it's great therapy but it would be nice to look at something I've painted and actually think, 'hey, that's pretty nice', instead of just 'there's that picture that got me through a shitty spell'.

I'm writing this and I'm thinking that maybe none of it's real – the Observatory, Andy, Cassie, Jay, Blackford, the helicopter, the plane, Hopkirk, the interview – that maybe this is some kind of *episode*. Like last November when Caroline found me curled up in the bottom of the shower, and she was screaming and trying to stop the bleeding, and I was like, "Just let me sleep, Caz. Just let me sleep. It's okay. I don't want to be so tired anymore." And later she was like, "I can't forgive you, Fi. I just can't." And then she was gone.

I start my 'task' tomorrow. Might be the distraction I need.

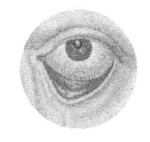

DIO Task Card for Andrew Keep:
REF: WI104/AK/Fauna

TASK OUTLINE
- Observe and catalogue any animal activity from Observation Deck 1 (marked 'Fauna').
- Limit your observations to what you can detect from the Observation Deck.
- Record your observations on the whiteboard immediately outside the Observation Deck.
- Ensure all recorded observations are as simple and clear as possible. Do not get hung-up on details.

EXAMPLES
- 'There were three squirrels today'
- 'A yellow bird made a nest'
- 'Something was moving in the trees but I don't know what it was'
- 'There were no animals today'

TASK SCHEDULE
Daily for 15 minutes at 0800 hours, 1100 hours, 1400 hours, 1700 hours, and 2000 hours.

IMPORTANT
Please wear the supplied white coat when carrying out tasks. This is mandatory.

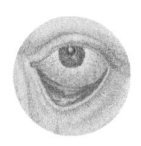

DIO Task Card for Cassandra Flint:
REF: WI104/CF/Flora
TASK OUTLINE

- Observe and catalogue any botanical activity from Observation Deck 2 (marked 'Flora').
- Limit your observations to what you can detect from the Observation Deck.
- Record your observations on the whiteboard immediately outside the Observation Deck.
- Ensure all recorded observations are as simple and clear as possible. Do not get hung-up on details.

EXAMPLES
- 'There are purple blossoms on one of the trees'
- 'The leaves on some of the trees are turning brown'
- 'The trees look unhealthy today'
- 'The trees are the same'

TASK SCHEDULE
Daily for 15 minutes at 0900 hours, 1200 hours, 1500 hours, 1800 hours, and 2100 hours.

IMPORTANT
Please wear the supplied white coat when carrying out tasks. This is mandatory.

DIO Task Card for Jagrav Panchal:
REF: WI104/JP/Weather

TASK OUTLINE
- Observe and catalogue any weather activity from Observation Deck 3 (marked 'Weather').
- Limit your observations to what you can detect from the Observation Deck.
- Record your observations on the whiteboard immediately outside the Observation Deck.
- Ensure all recorded observations are as simple and clear as possible. Do not get hung-up on details.

EXAMPLES
- 'It rained a lot today'
- 'There was a frost this morning'
- 'A mixture of sunshine and cloud'
- 'I did not care for the weather today'

TASK SCHEDULE
Daily for 15 minutes at 1000 hours, 1300 hours, 1600 hours, 1900 hours, and 2200 hours.

IMPORTANT
Please wear the supplied white coat when carrying out tasks. This is mandatory.

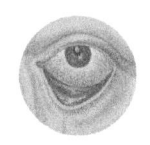

DIO Task Card for Fiona Needles:
REF: WI104/FN/Acoustics
TASK OUTLINE

- Observe and catalogue any acoustic activity from Observation Deck 4 (marked 'Acoustics').
- Limit your observations to what you can detect from the Observation Deck.
- Record your observations on the whiteboard immediately outside the Observation Deck.
- Ensure all recorded observations are as simple and clear as possible. Do not get hung-up on details.

EXAMPLES
- 'I could hear the rain striking the foliage'
- 'A bird was singing'
- 'There was thunder far away'
- 'Something shrieked in the forest'

TASK SCHEDULE
Daily for 15 minutes at 1100 hours, 1400 hours, 1700 hours, 2000 hours, and 2300 hours.

IMPORTANT
Please wear the supplied white coat when carrying out tasks. This is mandatory.

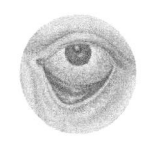

Random Audio Packet Transcript:
RAP/WI104/Day 0/1900-1901
Location: Recreation Area
Present: AK/CF/JP/FN

[00:00:00]
--starts--

Cassandra Flint: ... else think we're the subject of this experiment? It's actually us?

Jagrav Panchal: Hadn't crossed my mind [laughs] but, you know, *now* it has.

Cassandra Flint: It's like we've been dropped into a big petri dish.

Jagrav Panchal: [laughs].

Andrew Keep: It's clean enough. Feel like I'm dirtying the place up just sitting here.

Cassandra Flint: I mean, the stuff they've asked me... us to do doesn't... well it doesn't make any sense, does it? It's not science exactly is it? I have to write down what the... what the trees are doing and stuff like that, but I don't even know what types of trees they are.

Fiona Needles: (inaudible) and oak. I think.

Cassandra Flint: Maybe you should be doing trees [laughs]. I know fuck-all about them. What's your 'task'?

Fiona Needles: (inaudible).

Cassandra Flint: Acoustics? Should've brought my guitar. I know four chords [laughs].

Fiona Needles: (inaudible).

Andrew Keep: You could be right, there. They've got me on 'fauna' and I'm no David Bellamy.

Cassandra Flint: Who?

Andrew Keep: Botanist. Before your time.

Fiona Needles: (inaudible).

Andrew Keep: Yeah. Could be it's

--ends—
[00:01:00]

DAY ONE
COMPLEV 1

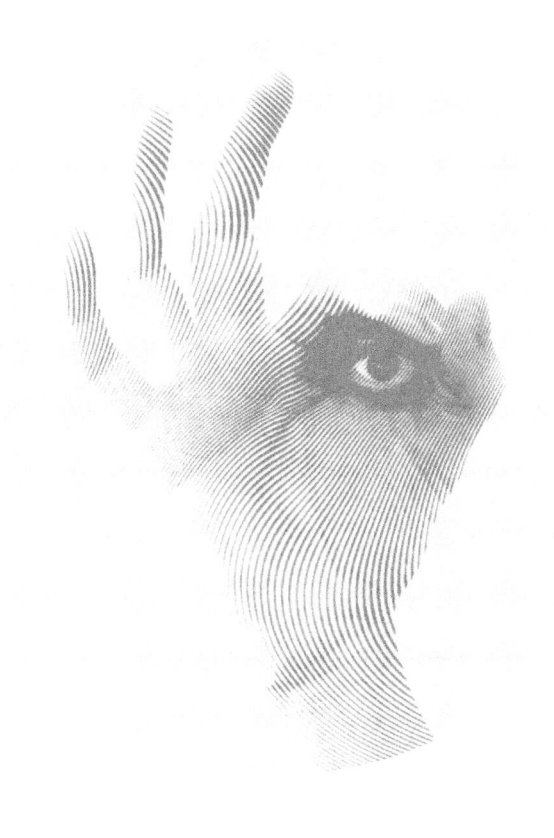

From the DIO Journal of Andrew Keep:

There's a record player in my room and a pile of LPs. It's all Stax and Motown. They didn't ask me about my musical tastes at the interview and it definitely wasn't in that weird questionnaire of theirs or that isometric test. Must have been snooping through my social media accounts. Which is creepy. But not as creepy as the alternative: flipping through our actual record collection in our actual house. They're original pressings too. *Green Onions*, *The Soul of a Bell*, *What's Goin' On*, and Otis Redding's *Soul Album*. I still can't listen to 'Cigarettes and Coffee' without you.

    I thought I'd miss you less once I was away from the house, but no. The tasks help a little. Fifteen minutes every hour of just looking out into the forest. So far, my sterling contributions to the advancement of scientific progress include 'A squirrel watched me from the nearest tree', 'A greyish bird with green tail feathers flew right by me' and (this one's going to set the world of scientific academia on fire) 'I think I saw a monkey but that can't be right. Maybe it was another squirrel'. The Nobel prize is in the bag, baby. In the bag.

    I heard some weird noises, too. Clicks and squeals. A bit like the sound of an old dial-up modem connecting to the internet or when you'd load Manic Miner onto your ZX Spectrum from a cassette. But not really like that at all, and so muted I wasn't sure if the sound was just in my own head. Remember that time I was being driven to distraction by that whistling noise and it turned out it was one of my own nostrils? Besides, Fiona's our resident acoustics expert. I wonder if they picked her because she speaks so quietly? Or maybe they picked her to balance out Cassie. She is LOUD. Not in a bad way, though. There's just a lot of personality going on in there. She's okay. Although… ninety days is a *long* time.

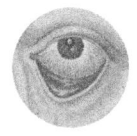

From the DIO Journal of Cassandra Flint:

I'm talking too much, I know, I know, I know. It's just nerves. Well, no, it's not *just* nerves, is it? It's that I'm not picking up anything. It's like the antenna in my head is broken. It's happened before when I've moved to a new school or a new apartment, sometimes even when I wear new clothes. Newness detunes me and it takes a while to find the right frequencies again. But there's always at least *something*. Here, there's nothing. Nothing.
I should know the name of someone's first pet by now without anyone saying a word. I should have a vague notion of whether Jag fancies Fiona or if Andy's a bit racist. I should have had glimpses of big events. Like if someone was in a car accident at some point or was mugged or got lost in a supermarket

when they were five or had a cancer scare.

I know these are real people, and if I was normal it wouldn't be an issue. But I'm not normal. I'm getting nothing, so it's like I'm interacting with three animated, physically convincing mannequins, but with nothing inside them but fibreglass and air pockets. It's not their fault, but they're creeping me the fuck out right now.

I thought I'd feel better once I was out on the balcony looking at the forest. But no. I mean I can see dirt and moss and what-have-you, can smell it on the air, but I can't *feel* it. I was going to write that on the whiteboard, 'I can't feel the forest', but I'm probably already getting on everyone's nerves and I don't want them thinking I'm some kind of headcase as well. So, I just wrote 'It's my first day. Nothing to report'.

It pisses me off that I'm following my mum's advice:

Nobody needs to know what's in your head, Cassandra. Keep it to yourself. Keep it to yourself and everyone will like you a whole lot more.

I could really go for a bit of weed right now. Just a pinch. Funny thing is weed *stops* me from receiving. It would make me feel exactly how I'm feeling now. But at least I'd know it was the weed causing interference and not the possibility that there's nothing out there to receive.

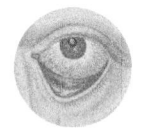

From the DIO Journal of Jagrav Panchal:

Fucking hell but I miss my iPhone. There's no technology here at all. No computers, tablets. Nothing. Even that radio on the top floor looks likes its full of valves and mouse droppings.

There are books in my room. Fucking books. Someone's taking the piss. Haven't read a book in years. Funny thing is, they're all old westerns. Louis L'Amor, Elmore Leonard, Zane Grey, Jack Schaefer, all the ones I used to read when I was a kid. I got them off my Uncle Harish, three carrier bags full of them. He said he got them from a house clearance in Feltham. I used to be well into them. Gave my parents hope, that did. Thought I was going to be a proper bookworm, studious and what-have-you. But I stopped reading them once I got an Xbox. And stopped playing on the Xbox once I got my iPhone.

If I had my phone I could take a selfie of me in my white coat. Mum and Dad would be delighted. I can imagine them at the temple.

"How's young Jagrav these days, aunty-ji?"

"Oh, he's a *scientist* now."

They don't need to know I'm not a *real* scientist. Just like they don't need to know I'm not a real property consultant. I mean, I am. Just not a very good one. I'm one step ahead of Aziz Khalid and his posse of leg-breakers because I made some very stupid investments on his behalf. They didn't seem like stupid investments at the time. But that's because, as I've just pointed out, I'm not very good at the property game. No idea what I'm good at, if I'm being completely honest. But it'll come to me. I'm entrepreneurial. I'll figure something out. If I don't fall foul of the likes of Khalid.

"How's young Jagrav these days, aunty-ji?"

"Oh, they found him floating in the Thames. They think someone caved his head in with a golf club."

This scientist lark isn't all it's cracked-up to be anyway. So far, the most interesting thing I've scribbled on the whiteboard is 'It looked like it was going to rain but then it didn't'.

"How's young Jagrav doing these days, aunty-ji?"

"Oh, he's a weatherman now. Regular Carol Kirkwood, he is. But a bloke. And brown."

Fucking hell. This has all got to be some kind of wind-up. I mean, *hasn't* it?

I miss my iPhone.

But I *really* miss Anjali. I was angry when she left, couldn't believe how she'd let me down, how badly she'd betrayed me. I mean, she left me on my own to face this shitstorm. How fucking *could* she? Now, it seems like she did the most sensible thing in the world. And, really, what choice did she have? Stick around, watch me get the shit beaten out of me or worse? Maybe get hurt herself? *Probably* get hurt herself? Did I really expect her to do that? Because if I did… what a *monumental* turd.

And let's be honest, I *was* a monumental turd. But maybe I'm not anymore. Or at least maybe I don't *have* to be. Maybe I'm a *recovering* monumental turd.

Yeah. I'll take that. It's not much, but it'll do for now. Until something better comes along.

From the DIO Journal of Fiona Needles:

I can't remember the last time I felt so relaxed. Except when I'm in the 'recreation area', obviously. When I'm there my anxiety kicks in, but so far not so much that I've needed my meds. But when I'm out on the balcony, it's like the best therapy I've ever had. It's like I've just done the biggest sneeze. At first, I didn't know what it was that was so soothing (and that's exactly what it is: *soothing*). I mean, I've been to forests before and they're always good places for me, but this is different. It took me a while to realise it's got nothing to do with the trees and the ferns and the shrubs and the ivy or even the fresh air. It's the fact that I have no idea where the nearest crowds are. Even when I was in the middle of nowhere, I'd know it was six miles to the next big town, ten to the next city, and the crowds were there, waiting.

Or maybe they'd come to me, just on whim, all of them, all the people, all at once. But this? I've no idea. Turns out ignorance *is* bliss.

I've started painting. I didn't *need* to. I *wanted* to. I just wanted to put some colour onto paper, make some shapes, create perspectives. The first couple were just abstracts, swirls of yellow and purple that might have been planets orbiting one another, lit by a single distant sun, if they had to be anything at all. The next couple were probably Caroline. They were certainly someone. Someone wearing white curled up sleeping like a cat on a Prussian sofa. It felt good to be painting for no reason other than to feel good.

I tried to sabotage this good feeling. Obviously. Why wouldn't I? It's what I do. During my first session on the balcony, I listened *so hard* because I wanted to pick up just a trace of traffic, the rumble of tyres on tarmac, the beep of a horn. Something to tell me there were people out there, maybe swarms of them, just out of sight. But there was nothing. Just birds singing, the wind rustling the leaves like someone flicking through a giant book, and the sound of old-school soul music coming from Andy's room below: "Nobody know how it grows and grows. Nobody knows it grows and grows..."

DAY TWO
COMPLEV 1

Random Audio Packet Transcript:
RAP/WI104/Day2/0710-0711
Location: Recreation Area
Present: AK/CF/JP/FN
[00:00:00]
--starts--

Cassandra Flint: ...not the weirdest dream I've ever had but it's definitely up there.

Jagrav Panchal: [laughs] Please, no. There's nothing worse than hearing about other people's dreams.

Cassandra Flint: Well, seeing as you've asked so nicely, Jag, I'll tell you.

Jagrav Panchal: [laughs]

Cassandra Flint: I was back in school but it wasn't my school it was... well more like... it was more like this place. It was all white and shiny and... too white and shiny. The teacher... he didn't have a face. It was just all smooth like an egg... and he was wearing a black suit like [laughs] at a funeral or like maybe a what-do-you-call-it an erm... an *undertaker*. Anyway, his head's basically [laughs] an... an egg so I don't know why I'm wittering on about his suit... And he's writing on a whiteboard but he's writing with a white pen so I can't see what it is that he's writing. And then—

Jagrav Panchal: Did you look down and see you weren't wearing any trousers? Mine, my dreams, are always like that. Like, like no trousers or being late for something. Or being late for something with no trousers.

Cassandra Flint: [laughs] No. His head split open

sort of where his mouth should have been... split open but there was no, you know, blood, and all this white, like, stringy stuff came out. Sort of like jellyfish stingers. And they
--ends--
[00:01:00]

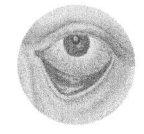

From the DIO Journal of Andrew Keep:

What was I supposed to say, Sarah? Yeah, Cassie, I had a dream just like that one, except I wasn't in school I was in a cave? A white cave like it was made of ice but it wasn't cold, so maybe it was quartz or something. And the bloke wasn't writing on a whiteboard, he was painting on the cave wall. But it was white-on-white so I had no idea what he was painting. Could have been a big cock and balls for all I know. But he was definitely an undertaker, the cave-painter. I've got quite a lot of very recent experience of those creepy bastards, so yes I recognised the profession right off the bat. I could smell him. Like vinegar. And yeah, just like in Cassie's dream, he had a head like an egg (goo goo g'joob) and it split open, only not from the mouth, but at the top, like a volcano erupting. But yeah, all this white stringy stuff. Yep, like jellyfish stingers. Like something you'd see trailing behind a

Portuguese man o' war. And no, I don't really think he was painting a big cock and balls. I thought, felt, like he was painting something *terrible* and I was glad I couldn't see it.

But, anyway. So What? Coincidence. Nothing to worry about. Except. Except we're *here*, in *this* place. The Observatory. None of us have a clue why we're here or why we're carrying out our 'tasks'. We've been told it's important and that we have to wear our white coats, but not why. "Why isn't important," Hopkirk said. But there was something in the way he said it – and I can't for the life of me pinpoint what – that told me that *he* didn't know why, that at some point he'd asked the same question (because why wouldn't you?) and he'd received the same answer: "Why isn't important."

But that nightmare... I don't mind telling you it scared me. Even before the jellyfish stingers started sprouting out all over the shop, I was scared.

Remember the nightmares you used to have, Sarah, when the chemo used to kick in? They were wild. Horrible and wild. You used to say they must have mixed-up your meds with a batch of bad acid and somewhere there was a hippy wondering why he felt like death and his hair was falling out. It's funny what you find funny when everything's fucking awful, isn't it?

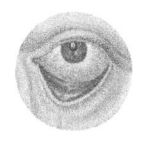

From the DIO Journal of Cassandra Flint:

I don't know why I kept laughing. I think I was trying to make light of it because it scared me more than I want to think about. And I lied. It was definitely the strangest dream I've ever had. And I didn't even mention some of the really fupped-duck details. Like the fact that I could *smell* the funeral guy. He smelled like weed. Good weed. A nice sativa weed, proper grassy. Like Brut Diesel or Basil Kush. Anyway, the important thing is I've never been able to smell anything in a dream before. I don't think anyone can, can they? It's like eating in a dream. Everything tastes of wet carboard. Or is that just me?

    Anyway, that wasn't the most fupped-duck thing. The most fupped-duck thing was that I didn't think it was *my* dream. I felt like I'd wandered into someone else's. Someone who could dream in scents and flavours.

    When I woke up, for a few seconds I couldn't move. When I did and sat up, my ears popped like I'd just come up from somewhere deep down where the pressure's too much. And not just deep down. Deep down and far away.

    It helped telling the others. Just getting it out of my head, I felt a bit better. Like when you've been feeling queasy for an hour and then up and out it comes and it's horrible but it's also kind of a relief.

    I'm starting to get a feel for this place now.

It's not as empty as it was on the first day. There *are* vibes. I don't know if they're coming from the building itself or from the others. I was brushing my teeth an hour or so ago and felt like a strip of silk rippled across the back of my neck. I nearly choked on Colgate foam. But it's a good thing, isn't it? Better than all that sanitised nothingness I thought I was going to have to put up with.

Going to watch Ace in the Hole. Kirk Douglas in front of the camera, Billy Wilder behind. Incredible. It wasn't much liked at the time. A critic for the New York Times, can't remember his name, said something about Wilder letting his imagination take over the story, so that it was distorted and grotesque. Well, quite. Isn't that the point?

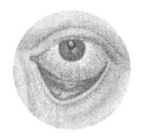

From the DIO Journal of Jagrav Panchal:

Usually my dreams are all in the naked-in-a-supermarket genre. Either that or Deepika Padukone and Samara Weaving getting gritty. Last night's was different. Don't know why I didn't say so when Cassie was rabbiting on. Suppose I didn't want to stray into her kooky-kitsch territory. I mean, we're like a sitcom here, aren't we? We've even got the set: sofas, armchairs, coffee table and a lamp. Cassie's the kooky one, Fiona's the timid one, I'm the good-looking go-getter (ha-ha) and Andy's the mid-life-crisis car-crash. Or something. Didn't say it was a good sitcom, did I?

Anyway, that dream. It was so similar to Cassie's, I was freaked-out for a bit. I wasn't in school. Well, not school-school. I was at a seminar in some high-rise boardroom. In The Shard or something. Everything was white. Even when I looked out of the windows, like there was a sky-high fog. There was a bloke in a natty navy pinstripe, proper Saville Row tailoring. But, like with Cassie's dream, he had no face. His head was just like a fucking egg. From the neck down, he was a geezer. From the collar up, a fucking nightmare. He was giving a PowerPoint presentation. There was an overhead projector hanging from the ceiling but no laptop or tablet. He had this thing in his left hand. About the size of a grapefruit. A cross between a heart and a lung, and bleached white. Every time he squeezed it, the slide would change. But all the slides were the same. Just white. Nothing on them. And then the heart-lung burst in his hand and all this stringy white stuff leaked out. Just like in Cassie's dream.

I'm thinking maybe it's like a Derren Brown stunt. You know, subliminal suggestion sort of thing? When they were interviewing us or when we were being given the tour, they said things to us, things that seemed innocuous at the time, things that we've all forgotten now but put ideas in our heads. The *same* ideas. Everything white, white-on-white, bursting white stringy things, pointless lectures, all that shit. I don't fucking know. Maybe that's the experiment. Maybe Cassie was right. It's us. We're the experiment. And there's a part of me that thinks 'So what?', if that's what it is, that's what it is. But there's part of me that's scared, too, because... what's in the next test tube?

I decided to take my mind off things with one of those western paperbacks. *The Tall Stranger* by Louis L'Amour. And it was like I was a kid again. Face in a book, not looking up, in another world. Even the smell of the thing – dry and dusty, old – was like a jolt of electricity going right into the part of my brain where the past lives. When I was a kid, Hounslow was not the most exciting place and my parents were pretty strict. They didn't like me and my brothers going out much. When I wasn't at school, I was at home or, sometimes, at the temple. But mostly at home. These books were a window to somewhere else and the stuff I saw through that window filled my head. I remember I used to go around saying 'Howdy' and 'Ma'am' and 'Reckon'. Until my older brother, Jayesh, told me I sounded like a cunt.

This book, *The Tall Stranger*, even *feels* like the one I had as a kid, the grain of it against my fingertips. It isn't. I know that because I drew a terrible picture in red biro of the main character, Rock Bannon, on the inside-front cover, and it isn't there. But it feels like it *should* be. It feels like I should be able to trace the indent of my drawing with my fingertips. But I can't. Obviously. That would be ridiculous, Derren Brown or not.

From the DIO Journal of Fiona Needles:

I suppose it didn't feel like a nightmare because there were no crowds. All of my nightmares are about football stadiums, shopping centres, protest marches. Crowds, crowds, crowds. This was just me and the egghead man. He scared me, don't get me wrong, but at least there was only one of him.

And his head didn't split open like in Cassie's dream. The top layer of skin peeled off and fell away, like a snake. What's that called? Sloughing? I think so. Like a snake sloughing its skin. And it kept doing that over and over. One layer after another. Like an onion. He was a snake-egg-onion man. A Sneggion. We were in a doctor's office, I think. Everything white. Except the Sneggion, he was wearing a serious suit, like something someone working for the civil service in the 1970s would wear. He wrote me a prescription. At least I think it was supposed to be a prescription. It was just a blank sheet of white paper. And, like in Cassie's dream, he wrote with a white pen, so I couldn't read what he'd prescribed me. Cipralex? Lustral? Seroxat? Efexor?

Weird that my dream was so like hers.
Coincidence?

I don't even like that word. Not after I found out that its 17th Century usage was 'occupies the same space'. That's what I think is at the core of my fear of crowds, my enochlophobia. It's not the fear of being crushed or suffocated, it's the sheer horror of finding myself occupying *precisely the same spot* as someone else. And not just occupying but *existing*, existing in precisely the same spot as someone else.

Or *something* else.

And why is that notion even in my head?

I've started painting again. The usual stuff. A tiny figure in the middle of nothing. A tiny me. And a grey smudge to represent a possible horizon hundreds of miles away.

I painted a couple of Carolines but then I thought… why? She's not coming back. You can't summon someone no matter how many paintings you make, Fiona. So, for now, it's just a lot of tiny Fionas in the middle of nothing and nowhere.

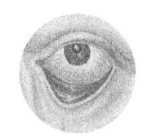

To: Carl Lyons
Subject: Random Audio Packet Transcript RAP/WI104/Day2/0710-0711
Attached: RAP-WI104-Day2-0710-0711.wav

Morning Sir,
I've attached this morning's RAP file.
I'm a little concerned about Flint's dream. Not recurring or shared but I thought it worth bringing to your attention.
Regards,
Ben Hopkirk
Project Administrator
Department of Incidents and Occurrences

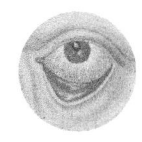

To: Ben Hopkirk
Subject: Re: Random Audio Packet Transcript RAP/WI104/Day2/0710-0711

Seems unlikely on Day 2. *Very* unlikely, in fact. Usually we're looking at around Day 30 before we see anything remotely like this. I'd put it down to coincidence. But let's err on the side of caution and take the Comprehension Level up a notch. And let's double the frequency of the RAPs. But, going forward, please stick to the Escalation Triggers as laid out in TO/WHP/WI/EscPro.v12. That is to say: Dreams (recurring or shared), Aggression (particularly unprovoked), Self-Harm, Hallucinations, Religiosity, Speaking in Tongues, Blistering, Other Voices.

Carl Lyons
Senior Project Manager
Department of Incidents and Occurrences

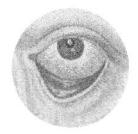

From the private journal of Ben Hopkirk:

Bumped into Sean McMahon as I was leaving work this evening. Haven't seen him for the better part of a year. He looked well. Still has a bit of a limp but not as bad as you'd expect given what happened to him. Went for a couple of pints at the Prince Alfred. We tried to avoid work-talk (protocol and everything) but he told me a few rumours he'd been hearing about Lyons. Said he's got a well-concealed drink problem and his eye's off the ball more than it's on. Said he's got leverage, though, so they can't replace him. Something about having dirt on Project Director Kendall. Can't say all of this doesn't worry me. At least we've raised the CompLev. Don't know what that means exactly but it feels like we're taking things a bit more seriously.

Popped into see Dad. He was watching an old episode of *Only Fools and Horses* in the lounge. I say watching. More like staring in the general direction of the telly. At one point though, he was staring *hard*, like he was trying to see *through* the screen, past it, to whatever lives on the other side. I was about to ask him what it was, what was he seeing, but then one of the other residents had a proper shrieking freak-out and my dad closed his eyes and I got the fuck out of there.

Be interesting to see what's in the next RAP file. Christ, I hope Flint doesn't start talking about dreams again. I already think Lyons is losing patience with me and I've hardly fucking troubled the man. I just want the rest of this Iteration to be uneventful.

DAY THREE
COMPLEV 2

Random Audio Packet Transcript:
RAP/WI104/Day3/1515-1516
Location: Recreation Area
Present: AK/JP/FN
[00:00:00]
--starts--
Andrew Keep: Nippy out there.
Jagrav Panchal: Yeah. Brass monkey weather.
Andrew Keep: Yeah.
Fiona Needles: Yeah.
[silence 00:00:32]
Andrew Keep: Yeah. Bloody cold. Bloody cold.
[silence 00:00: 17]
Jagrav Panchal: We should put this conversation forward for some kind of award.
[laughter]
--ends--
[00:01:00]

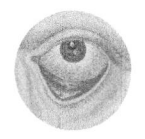

From the DIO Journal of Andrew Keep:

No chemo dreams last night, Sarah. At least none that I remember. And I'm pretty sure I'd remember if I'd had them. Mustn't have slept well, though. Really tired. Couldn't concentrate when I was out on the Observation Deck. Thought I saw something in the woods, something tall and skinny and white. Sort of like a man but not really. One second it was there and then it was gone. Maybe it was just a loose scrap of mist. That's kind of what it looked like. Anyway, I didn't put it on the whiteboard.

Got talking to Fiona last night. She set the ball rolling. Cassie was out on floral duties so Fiona could actually get a word in for once. She asked me why I was here, at The Observatory. It took me by surprise because no-one's asked that yet, and it kind of seemed like an unspoken rule. A *Fight Club* thing. Jagrav looked at me and raised his eyebrows like she'd just asked me if I was gay or if I'd put on weight. Funny thing is, I just answered her. Didn't think twice about it. I told her everything. I told her about you. About what happened. About our happy-go-lucky lifestyle, taking each day as it comes, and how that was working like a charm until Cancer decided we were far *too* happy and were desperately in need of being fucked over, and hard. I told her how quickly everything had collapsed. The debt, the bad pension, the insurance policy that wouldn't pay out, and how I borrowed money to tide me over until the policy *did* pay out. Only it didn't. It fucking didn't because the world is full of venal, avaricious sociopaths who are incapable of seeing the connection between their mindless acquisitiveness and the fact that there are people who can't keep their head above the waterline no matter how hard they kick, no matter how hard they work. These rapacious bastards can't see the stinking sticky stuff connecting their rooftop swimming pool to some guy withering away in Shithole, Lancashire, who can't eat *and* pay his rent.

Anyway, I digress. I di-fucking-gress.

I felt better for it. For getting all that shit out. For lancing that boil. And, maybe it was because I looked like I felt better for it, relieved, that Jagrav told us his story.

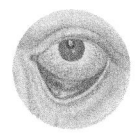

From the DIO Journal of Jagrav Panchal:

It was only when I started telling Fiona and Andy how badly I'd fucked-up, telling them about when Aziz Khalid's boys turned up at my flat not just with golf clubs but in *full golfing attire*, that it really occurred to me just how much shit I'd dropped myself into. More than that, I felt properly scared for the first time. I mean, I'd been scared when those goons showed up. But it was normal fear. Sensible fear. This was bigger. It went through me like an electric shock, from somewhere around the back of my neck right down to the tips of my toes. Shit, I even felt it in my balls.

I mean, they were going to put me in a hospital bed or a wheelchair or a ditch. Suddenly, I could see it, see them, see Khalid and his henchmen lurching toward me, teeth bared, eyes bloodshot, knuckles white. I could see the light glinting off the shafts of their Callaway Strata nine irons. I could hear Anjali crying. It was real. It was very fucking real.

But there was another fear. Underneath the real fear of Khalid. It was a different kind of fear, shifting and oily. This wasn't the fear of having my shins splintered with a nine iron. This was… I don't know what it was. It reminded me of the time I was in India with my mum when I was about eleven or twelve and we went into this little roadside shrine, just outside Patna I think it was. The moment we were in there, my mum turned around and ushered me out. She was scared. "Baahar jao! Baahar jao!" And I saw, just over her shoulder, a statue of Kali, in the dark, lit by a grainy shaft of sunlight probing in through a hole in the roof. Kali's tongue was hanging down past her chin and she was wearing a necklace of skulls. It wasn't a very well-made statue. It was all peeling and warped and distorted, like it had been made from plaster and the damp and humidity had got into it. Anyway, there must have been rainwater as well as sunlight coming in through the roof, dripping onto the statue, because it looked like there was drool dripping off her tongue and her eyes glistened.

I'd forgotten all about that.

Why am I remembering it now?

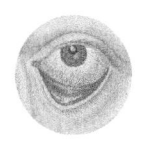

From the DIO Journal of Fiona Needles:

I honestly thought Jag was going to cry, and that was the only reason I started talking. I've never known what to do when men cry. I always think that maybe they hope you don't notice, so it's best to pretend you haven't. So I started talking about my enochlophobia. Like most people, Jag and Andy seemed to struggle with the idea that a phobia can just come out of nowhere. I tried to explain it to them, how there doesn't have to be a root cause or a trigger, but I think they still secretly think I was in some kind of horrible crowd-related incident that I've blocked out of my memory because it was so awful.

But it did just happen. Twenty-seven years old and I suddenly couldn't handle being in crowds. And then I couldn't handle even the prospect of being in crowds. And then the very idea that there might be a crowd somewhere out there just waiting for me planted a flag in my consciousness.

And it fucked up everything. Relationships, friendships, jobs, even family. Everybody lost patience with me. Christ, who wouldn't? Even I lost patience with me. I remember, one time, my therapist looking at me with absolute withering contempt when she thought I was looking past her out the window. Or maybe I imagined that because I wanted her to be contemptuous of me, because I didn't want her understanding, anyone's understanding, because being understood would be like being known and I didn't want that. I don't know why I didn't want that, but I didn't. I think I've always been that way, My mum called me secretive, but I really wasn't. I think I was just striving for some sort of invisibility.

But I don't think that's just me, is it? Nobody really wants to be watched and have things written about them on a whiteboard, do they?

Jag was saying that some people want nothing but to be seen. That's *all* they want, eyes on them and for everyone to know what they are. I said, "Like who?" and he said, "I don't know. People. Things."

"Things?" I said. And he said, "I don't know why I said that." He looked really confused for a minute. Like he didn't know who he was, where he was, what was going on. Like someone with dementia.

From the DIO Journal of Cassandra Flint:

I keep getting that silk-across-the-neck feeling. Especially when I'm out on the observation deck. I'm picking up something else too. A voice. At first, I thought it was Fiona. The quiet ones always transmit the loudest. But now I don't know. I don't know who it is. Maybe it's just something I'm remembering. That's what it's like being sensitive. Sometimes you think you're getting something but really it's just one of your own memories crawling up out of the past. This might be that. Could be my sister, the voice. Could even be me. It was a game we used to play when we were kids. What's the time, Mr. Wolf? That's what the voice seems to be saying. "What's the time, Mr. Wolf?" I hated that game. Being Mr. Wolf was the worst. People creeping up on you while your back's turned. Some stressful shit.

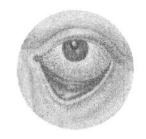

Random Audio Packet Transcript:
RAP/WI104/Day3/0130-0131
Location: Recreation Area
Present: N/A
[00:00:00]
--starts--
[silence 00:00:27]
[footsteps 00:00:08]
[silence 00:00:14]
[high-pitched whine 00:00:11]
--ends--
[00:01:00]

DAY FOUR
COMPLEV 2

Random Audio Packet Transcript:
RAP/WI104/Day4/1320-1321
Location: Recreation Area
Present: AK/CF/JP/FN
[00:00:00]
--starts--

Andrew Keep: ...really not bad.
Jagrav Panchal: Better than Pot Noodle.
Andrew Keep: Yeah... You want one, Cassie? I'm a wizard with boiling water and a fork. Just ask Jag.
Jagrav Panchal: Yeah. A fucking culinary wizard.
Cassandra Flint: Sorry?
Andrew Keep: One of these packet-noodle-things? Want one? They're posh.
Cassandra Flint: No thanks. Not hungry.
Andrew Keep: Fiona?
Fiona Needles: Not for me, thanks. Just had a sandwich. Thanks, though.
Andrew Keep: If you're sure... But you're really missing out. Get a load of these ingredients. It's got all your daily essentials. Potassium carbonate, sodium carbonate, maltodextrin, onion powder, potassium chloride, monosodium glutamate, disodium in... inosinate? Disodium... guany-something-or-other. Can't even pronounce that one. And it's got mushroom juice concentrate. Lovely stuff, that, mushroom juice concentrate. How can you resist?
Cassandra Flint: [laughs] Sounds delicious but—
[loud crackling noise]
Andrew Keep: What the fuck was

--ends--
[00:01:00]

To: Carl Lyons
Subject: Random Audio Packet Transcript RAP/WI104/Day4/1320-1321
Attached: RAP-WI104-Day4-1320-1321.wav
Morning Sir,
Given the way in which this afternoon's RAP file concluded, would it be prudent to open a live audio stream?
Regards,
Ben Hopkirk
Project Administrator
Department of Incidents and Occurrences

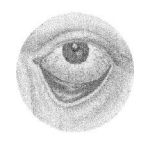

To: Ben Hopkirk
Subject: Re: Random Audio Packet Transcript RAP/WI104/Day4/1320-1321
I appreciate your concern, Ben, and your enthusiasm is to be commended, but live streaming must always be a last resort (as per paragraph 31 of TO/WHP/WI/EscPro.v12). Let's just see what the

next Audio Packet gives us.
Carl Lyons
Senior Project Manager
Department of Incidents and Occurrences

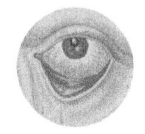

From the DIO Journal of Andrew Keep:

How did nobody else see it? It was like the thing I saw in the woods yesterday. Tall, white, skinny, fast-moving. Like the thing in the woods but this time it was definitely *there*, and it was moving across the recreation area. It was the shape of a long early-morning shadow but upright, perpendicular to the floor, and made of something like steam or maybe really fine silk. To be honest, Sarah, I don't really know if that's what it looked like at all. It feels like my mind's trying to come up with the closest approximation it can to something that it really isn't able to frame.

By the time Jagrav says "What?" the thing's gone, down the spiral staircase to the ground floor.

"Didn't you see that?" I said. For some reason I was asking Cassie. Don't know why. I just thought of everyone there she was the one more likely to have seen it.

"See what?" she said.

I just pointed to the staircase, even though the

thing had already wound down out of sight.

"That man," I said, and I didn't know why I said that because it was just skinny blurs really. Were there arms and legs? A Head? Maybe.

I followed it down the stairs, but there was nothing there. I went outside and walked around the perimeter of the Observatory. Nothing. By the time I got back to the rec area, I was beginning to think I hadn't really seen it at all, that it was just an optical illusion. Only not even that. It was just… nothing. I hadn't seen anything. None of it had happened.

And I honestly didn't think about it again until I started writing in my journal twenty minutes ago. And now both ideas seem to exist at the same time, overlapping on the same spot, the idea that it was nothing and I didn't really see it and that it was very real and I very definitely did see it. It makes me feel nauseous and scattered. It makes me want to use the radio on the second floor and call for help, but I don't know why, or even what I would say.

If I see it again, I'm following it. Wherever it goes, I'm going to follow it. Even though it scares me. *Because* it scares me. Even though it won't be there.

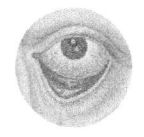

From the DIO Journal of Cassie Flint:

It's almost all the time, that silk-across-the-neck feeling. And the voice. "What's the time, Mr. Wolf?" Don't know who it is. Not Fiona, I'm pretty sure of that.

I keep seeing things, too, just out of the corner of my eye and only for a second or two. Like fog but trying to be a person and not very good at it.

I tried to watch a little bit of *Spellbound*, but I was asleep before Rhonda Fleming is summoned to Ingrid Bergman's office. I woke up very briefly to Gregory Peck's John Ballantyne declaring, "I'm haunted, but I can't see by what!" And then I was asleep again. Or half asleep. I thought I could hear Ballantyne's declaration as if it was stuck on a loop. "I'm haunted, but I can't see by what!" Over and over. Round and round.

From the DIO Journal of Jagrav Panchal:

Don't know what's wrong with everyone today. Cassie and Andy are so fucking jumpy, and Fiona's the opposite, she's gone back to being what she was like when we all got here, like she's trying to make herself far away, and I don't even know what I mean by that.

Fell asleep this afternoon and when I woke

up, Kali was there. Kali from the roadside shrine near Patna. She was standing at the foot of my bed, all peeling paint and bloated plaster, water dripping from her tongue. I could hear each drop as it hit the floor. Tap. Tap. Tap. I could smell India and I could feel the humidity. It was like I had to open my eyes three or four times before I was awake and she was gone.

Fucking Kali. In my fucking bedroom.

I'm almost certain Cassie was right now. We're the experiment. Maybe they've put something in those posh Fortnum & Mason Pot Noodles. Maybe it's in the mushroom juice concentrate.

I tried to read one of the westerns before bed. *Silver Canyon* by Louis L'Amour. But I couldn't get more than a few pages through it. Certain words kept jumping out at me. It was as if the type was bigger and bolder, except when I'd look again it wasn't. And it was always the same words. 'Know'. 'Understand'. 'See'.

I put the book down and tried to sleep but every time I closed my eyes, I heard my dad reading from one of the Hindu scriptures. No, I don't remember which one because I'm a fucking coconut, aren't I? He was saying, "When the atman is in the land of dreams, then all worlds belong to that atman." And he was saying it over and over. I don't even remember my dad being that religious to be honest. I certainly don't remember him reading from the Vedas or Upanishads or what-have-you. We'd go to the temple for the big occasions – Diwali,

Holi, Krishna Janmashtami – but that was pretty much it. We were about as Hindu as your average white family are Christian. That is to say, pretty much not at all.

So, why all this? Why all this God stuff?

Anyway. Tired now.

From the DIO Journal of Fiona Needles:

I can feel the crowd. I can't hear it or see it, but I can feel it. I can feel it occupying the same space as me. Not fully. I'd be screaming now if that was the case. But in a *thin* way. In a *ghost* way. And not all the time. It comes and it goes.

Painting isn't helping. The usual tiny figure in the middle of nothing seems to be surrounded, or even *overlapped*, by countless invisible somethings. Listening to Andy's music helps a little. When I was out on the Observation Deck, my last shift, I could hear Otis Redding coming up from Andy's room. *Scratch My Back*. I focused on the song. What was the point of listening to the forest? It never made any interesting sounds anyway. Just birds and leaves, sometimes rain. It can't really compete with Otis Redding, that *voice*, or with those trumpets, with Wayne Jackson, Sammy Coleman Bowlegs Miller. I didn't know who any of these people where or what they did before coming to The Observatory, but Andy's like a Stax and Motown Wikipedia. He knows who played on what record when, and he likes to share his knowledge. Jag calls him the Pub Bore, but I find it interesting. I mean, there's the song and then there's the story behind the song. The how and why of it, the history. Anyway, *Scratch My Back* fades out and *Treat Her Right* starts up. For a while it's all good, I'm just listening to the record, staring out into the forest, which is so dark I can't see a damn thing anyway even if I *did* hear something, but then the needle starts jumping and skipping. And it's not randomly skipping. It keeps repeating the same phrases, like a clumsy attempt at sampling.

"... tell you a story... ought to know... real... know... tell you a story... ought to know... real... know... tell you a story... ought to know... real... know..."

It does this over and over, round and round. It was hypnotic and I kind of lost track of time. I was about to go back in, to see if Andy's okay, when the record suddenly jumped to *Everybody Makes a Mistake* and we're back on track.

Something must have bitten me while I was out on the Observation Deck. Little lumps all over the back of my left hand, like the beginnings of blisters. Itchy. I'll get something for it. There's a pretty good first aid kit in the rec area. Bound to have some calamine lotion, antihistamines, a hacksaw.

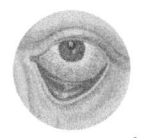

Random Audio Packet Transcript:
RAP/WI104/Day4/0015-0016
Location: Recreation Area
Present: AK/FN
[00:00:00]
--starts--
Fiona Needles: … that… that you, Andy?
[silence 00:00:12]
Fiona Needles: Andy?
[silence 00:00:11]
Andrew Keep: Go back to bed, Fiona. Nothing to worry about.
Fiona Needles: I used to sleepwalk.
Andrew Keep: I'm not… Yeah. Okay. Goodnight, Fiona.
Fiona Needles: Can you hear people, Andy?
Andrew Keep: No… Well, there's you, obviously.
Fiona Needles: I mean lots of people.
Andrew Keep: Still just you, Fiona.
Fiona Needles. Okay… Goodnight.
Andrew Keep: Goodnight. See you in the morning.
[footsteps]
--ends--
[00:01:00]

DAY FIVE
COMPLEV 2

Random Audio Packet Transcript:
RAP/WI104/Day5/1040-1041
Location: Recreation Area
Present: CF/JP/FN
[00:00:00]
--starts--
Jagrav Panchal: … seen Andy?
Fiona Needles: Last night. He was here.
Jagrav Panchal: Today, though.
Cassie Flint: Have you checked his balcony?
Jagrav Panchal: No.
Cassie Flint: Probably there, then.
Jagrav Panchal: Probably.
[silence 00:00:28]
Cassie Flint: Whose turn is it to make a brew?
Jagrav Panchal: Yours.
Cassie Flint: Bollocks. I got the last one in.
Jagrav Panchal: Definitely yours, Cass.
Cassie Flint: Fiona? Tell him he's talking bollocks.
Fiona Needles: Usually I'd agree, but it's definitely your round, Cassie.
Cassie Flint: Is it? Maybe it is. Mind's a bit of a shithole at the moment.
Fiona Needles: Yeah.
Cassie Flint: I know this is a longshot [whispering] but has anyone got any… weed?
[laughter]
--ends—
[00:01:00]

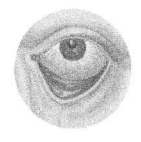

From the DIO Journal of Andrew Keep:

Sarah. I don't know where to start. Or maybe I do, and I just don't want to. You know me: prevaricate until the problem goes away. What did you say my family motto should be? 'Dither for days, do nothing and doze'. Something like that. Anyway, you said that was just fine, because you were a ditherer and a dozer, too.

I found a journal. Not like this one. It was put together from old bits of stationary and cereal packets and sewn together with bootlaces. It was covered in... I don't know what it was covered in. Stinks. Some of it's printed-out emails, official documents, some of it looks like it's been scrawled by a complete fucking lunatic. And it all *sounds* like it's been scrawled by a complete fucking lunatic. Even the emails, the 'official' bits. Fucking hell, Sarah. Fucking hell. Should I tell the others? Should I use the radio, call for help? But who would I be talking to? Whoever it was, they'd know. They'd already know about Percipience. Wouldn't they? Or is that the whole point? Fuck. My head's a mess, a complete mess. My mind feels like... I don't know what it feels like. Fistfuls of jelly squeezing out between finger gaps.

I don't even know why I went out on the

Observation Deck when I did. It wasn't my shift. I just knew I'd see something. Just knew. Because the record was jumping? Telling me? Telling me that I ought to know. Ought to know the real story? And there he was. *It* was. The Steam Man. Only not a man. The Steam *Thing*. On the edge of the forest, waiting for me. That's what it felt like anyway, like it was waiting. It was moving the whole time, slithering between the trees, but somehow, at the same time, it was still and waiting.

I bumped into Fiona as I was making my way to the stairs and I *almost* let that little encounter convince me not to go, like it was a sign or something. Christ, I wish I'd listened to that little knot in my stomach that said "stay". I wish I didn't know anything. Not knowing, you see, that's how we survive.

But I didn't stay. I went out into the woods and I followed the Steam Thing.

Damn thing couldn't make its mind up. One minute it would be moving slowly, letting me keep up, the next it would move so quick it was like a speeded-up film, jittery, jerky and then gone. I'd wander in circles thinking I'd lost it (fuck me, *relieved* that I'd lost it) and then it would show up again, a thin, stringy cloud of what? The more I looked at it, the more the forest around me started to seem unnatural. Not just unnatural: unreal. Even the temperature. It wasn't warm or humid, like it was on the first day. It wasn't cold, either. It wasn't anything. It was more like when you stay in the bath just a little too long and the water matches your own body temperature and you can't feel the water anymore unless you move. The trees looked dry and dead, the bark warped and cracked, but the leaves and needles were fat and rubbery and glistening with moisture. The ground was spongey beneath my feet, like layers and layers of thick carpet drawn not-quite-tight over a gaping hole. And I couldn't smell anything except myself.

There were no animals. I wondered what I'd write on the whiteboard, then I remembered two of the examples from my task card: 'Something was moving in the trees but I don't know what it was' and 'There were no animals today'. I imagined myself writing 'There was nowhere for the animals to be today because the forest had become something else'.

Sometimes I couldn't tell if I was going uphill or down. I'd be scrabbling up a slope, pulling myself along with vines or arching roots that felt like they were made of half-defrosted meat, the Steam Thing above me about to disappear over some ridge or other, and then I'd be tumbling, head-over-fucking-heels. That happened at least, what? Four or five times? No, more. Lots more. I don't know. I started to feel sick, so I just lay there with my eyes closed. You know when you've had too much to drink and you go to bed and every time you close your eyes it's like you're on the waltzers at a dodgy travelling fairground and you have to sit up and take a couple of deep breaths? It was like that. Except when I sat up, there wasn't any slope for me to have rolled down or clambered up. Everything was flat and there were no trees for at a least a couple of hundred yards.

I was in the middle of what looked like a blast zone, only it wasn't a crater like that Siberian one, like Tunguska. It was just flat. It wasn't like something had struck the Earth, a meteor or what-have-you. It was like some force had pulsed outward from where I was standing and neatly levelled everything. There were no tree stumps. There was no debris at all. There was just the same spongey ground as before, a carpet of dirt with nothing beneath it. It felt like it could all come loose at any second and plunge downward and wrap around me, sending me to wherever in a dirt-carpet cocoon.

Christ, Sarah, I really don't know how to tell this story, what order to put the events in, how to lay out the facts so it pulls together into something at least approximating a coherent account.

For a second, I didn't know how I'd got there. It wasn't that I'd forgotten the Steam Thing, it was that none of it had happened. I *knew* none of it had happened, not even the Observatory or any of that stuff. I was just there for no reason. And then – and this is really fucked-up – I was at home, standing halfway upstairs with a cup in one hand, a plate in the other, saying, "Shit. I was supposed to take these into the kitchen. Loosing my marbles, Sarah." And then I heard you laugh from the living room, and you said, "Already lost them, love. Think there's a few down the back of the sofa, a couple under the fridge, but that's about it for you and marbles, sweetheart."

I started crying, and then I was back in the clearing, the blast zone. I saw the Steam Thing at the edge of the forest, directly ahead of me, and I got to my feet, grunting like the old fart I am, and headed toward it, wiping my eyes. I honestly have no idea how long it took me to get there. Honestly no idea. But I was breathing hard on that same-temperature-as-me air when I got there, by which time it had gone. Of course it had. Because this was all a fucking game. Chase. Catch. Tag. Or an entirely new recreational activity called 'Let's Fuck with Andy Keep's Sanity for Shits and Giggles'.

Then I saw the bivouac. It was made out of those dead, cracked trees with their somehow-still-alive leaves, and just about big enough for one person, maybe two at a squeeze.

I didn't go in for a long time.

I don't think I've ever been so scared. Except maybe when we were in the hospital, waiting to see the doctor about your results – *our* results – when we'd just known they were going to be bad, the worst, but had been pretending to each other and ourselves that everything was going to be fine, just fine, just fucking *dandy*, dandy as a dandelion. It had been like waiting to be executed, hadn't it? One of us said that later, I can't remember who because we'd had so much to drink, every drop of booze we'd managed to pull together from every cupboard in the house, even the Advocaat, poured into pint glasses. "A Filthy Cocktail" you'd called it. "It's filthy cocktail hour!" you'd declared, holding your glass up high, and we'd knocked back something that was like fermented cough medicine, lighter fuel and Vimto. Christ but it'd done the trick, though, hadn't it? We didn't sober-up for days.

Christ, I need a drink. I'd even go a couple of shots of Advocaat and what even is that weird yellow shit?

It reeked inside the bivouac. It smelled like something had died in there. And probably something had. There was only one bone, sat on top of a sodden sleeping bag. Could have been a thigh bone. Could have been human. I don't know. There was most of a once-white lab coat, hanging from the inside of the ridge of the bivouac. It was torn here and there as if whoever had been wearing it had been attacked, clawed by a wild animal. But there was no blood. That and the bone were the only indications that something violent might have taken place here. Except for the smell. Like death. A metastatic stink. I know that smell.

I unzipped the sleeping bag and opened it up. It felt like surgery, like I was carrying out an autopsy, peeling back a layer of flesh. There was a man-shaped stain. A Shroud-of-Turin sort of a stain. It was like mildew, but shimmery. I wasn't sure if that shimmeriness was a property of the stain or something wrong with my eyes.

Anyway, in the sleeping bag, wrapped in wet

polythene, was the journal. The old-stationery-and-cereal-packets-bound-with-bootlaces journal.

On the cover – a slab of fat, water-stained-and-warped cardboard – written in thick marker, was, 'Percipience'.

FROM THE PERCIPIENCE JOURNAL

To: Jonathan Kendall
Subject: Concerns

Good morning Mr. Kendall,

Let me begin by apologising for 'breaking the chain of command'. It's possible you're aware of my numerous attempts to convince my immediate line manager, Doctor Collins, of my concerns regarding events at South Atlantic 37.45.12.70. It's also possible you may share his opinion that I'm creating a fuss over nothing. However, I have a duty of care and feel it would be remiss of me not to, at least, attempt to take this issue higher.

The increase in 'religiosity' here at the research station is unsettling to say the least, especially given the atheistic nature of all of the scientific personnel and indeed most of the ancillary staff. When someone as nullifidian as Professor Adebayo begins talking about "being guided by Orunmila" (a Yoruba spirit of wisdom and divination) I think we need to consider what psychological effects the Obscurity might be having on its observers.

And then there's the matter of the shared dreams. 'The Faceless Thing That Strains to Teach' as Professor Adebayo calls it. Granted, there's every possibility that people are influencing one another's dreams unconsciously by talking about the contents of their own (chicken or egg?) but I think it's worth factoring this 'phenomenon' into your considerations.

Regards,
Natalie McCluskey

Senior Occupational Safety and Wellbeing Officer
Department of Incidents and Occurrences

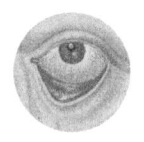

To: Natalie McCluskey
Subject: Re: Concerns
Thank you, Natalie. Keep me informed.
Regards,
Jonathan Kendall
Project Director
Department of Incidents and Occurrences

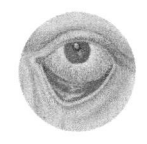

To: Jonathan Kendall
Subject: Serious Health Concerns
Good morning Mr. Kendall,
There can be no doubt that the blisters many of the staff are suffering from (myself included) can only be as a result of exposure to the Obscurity. Doctor Collins is wilfully misunderstanding me on this matter and continues to reference the safe levels of radiation at the research station. He knows full well that I have no concerns about radioactivity. The Obscurity has hardly any physical presence at all. The risks it poses are all psychological and, now,

with the addition of this outbreak of blistering, psychosomatic. The blistering seems to present more aggressively in those who have had some success in the analysis of data gathered from the Obscurity (Sullivan, Henderson, Benton and Walsh).
Regards,
Natalie McCluskey
Senior Occupational Safety and Wellbeing Officer
Department of Incidents and Occurrences

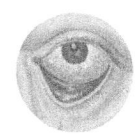

To: Natalie McCluskey
Subject: Re: Serious Health Concerns
Thank you, Natalie. Please continue to follow the agreed protocols and work closely with Dr. Campbell with regard to potential biohazards. Keep me informed of any further developments.
Regards,
Jonathan Kendall
Project Director
Department of Incidents and Occurrences

To: Jonathan Kendall
Subject: Violence and Self-Harm

Good evening Mr. Kendall,

I'm not sure if you'll pick this up until the morning. I hope you're working late.

The outbreaks of violence continue. Again, the common denominator is *knowing*. The most violent are those who have processed the most data and, in particular, those who have begun to identify patterns and build models. Henderson, who is now head-to-toe in blisters, has had to be restricted to quarters because he will almost certainly kill someone. Conversely, those who have had little luck with their data are displaying a variety of troubling symptoms, including insomnia, anhedonia and psychomotor agitation. Professor Dodwell with all of her talk of quantum yields and photoacoustic microscopy has successfully gathered no data whatsoever and is in a state of almost continuous suicidal ideation. She's under 24-hour watch now, for her own safety.

Doctor Collins assures me measures are being taken to [remainder of page illegible due to staining].

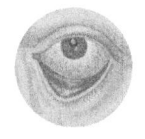

To: Jonathan Kendall
Subject: Percipience
[illegible due to staining] gone now. Just mildew left behind. Dodwell was right. We must not know The Obscurity. It must remain obscure. It exists outside

of our current paradigms. To understand it is to *admit* it. In both senses of the word: to acknowledge or accept as valid and to allow someone, something, to gain access. The sentence that begins 'The Obscurity is' must remain forever unfinished. And even this, I fear, is too much of an understanding. Could even knowing that it must remain unknown, that it is desperate to *be* known, be enough to take the Obscurity from *there* to *here*? Am I teaching you to destroy the universe, Jonathan? Or are you even there? Is everything gone already? Has the Obscurity arrived? Blackford ran to the helicopter as soon as it landed. He said he wouldn't. Said he understood, that he'd hide like me. We know too much to go back. We're part of the problem now. We're holes in the fabric of our paradigm, holes through which the Obscurity might *squeeze*. Is it already squeezing? Has it already squozen?
Regards,
Natalie McCluskey
Senior Occupational Safety and Wellbeing Officer
Department of Incidents and Occurrences

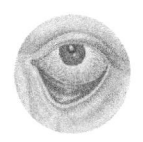

To: Jonathan Kendall
Subject: Steam!
They are not dead. Collins, Sullivan, Henderson, Benton, Walsh, Adebayo all of them. They are steam.

White wisps. Barely there. Thin voices. They are, I believe, packets of data. They are a fragile membrane of what they remember of themselves containing what they know of the Obscurity. This is [remainder of page illegible due to staining].

To: Jonathan Kendall
Subject: What's the time, Mr. Wolf?
That's the game we must play, isn't it? What's the time, Mr. Wolf? We must turn and look. If it is seen, it is still. It is when we look away that it creeps up on us. But we must not understand it or there will be nothing left of us but mildew and steam. Of course, it isn't a wolf. It's a god. Possibly even God. Its arrival is our end. There isn't enough room, you see. Soon, I will [illegible due to staining]. Or is it Proud Lucifer? Does it demand we look upon it, admire it? Is it dangerous when dismissed, when it is unadmired? Must we clothe ourselves in the white coats of our trade and feign scientific curiosity and unscientific awe? [illegible due to staining] have to reassure the Wolf, make it think it has our attention. We must look without seeing, observe without analysis, stare and stare and stare but never see, never know. Never let it in. Not by the hairs on my chinny chin chin.

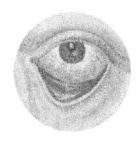

Handwritten Notes:
What's the time, Mr. Wolf?
One o'clock.

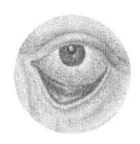

Handwritten Notes:
What's the time, Mr. Wolf?
Why, gosh. It's 13.7-billion years later.

Handwritten Notes:
What's the [illegible due to staining]. The sun is going down. How am I doing? There's a sense that I'm not dying, rather I am ceasing to be separate. It's cold out here in the woods at night and [illegible due to staining]. Nobody has come to find me. I think I would have heard a helicopter. When I was seven, my dad took me to the Biggin Hill aerodrome for an air show. A sightseeing helicopter struck the underside of a de Havilland Tiger Moth. Five people died. I can still remember the sound: crunching,

scraping. The crowd made the same ooh! sounds as they did when the planes were doing their stunts, as if it were all equally entertaining. It was on the news, on the telly. Me and my dad were in the background. I had pigtails and Dad still had hair and was alive.

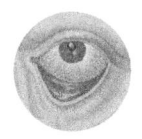

Handwritten Notes:
What's the time, Mr. Wolf?
What even *is* time? The arrow of time cannot be found in the Laws of Physics. We experience it, the messy omelette of existence, but it is not there in the mechanics of the Universe.

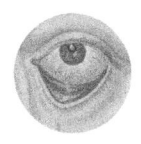

Handwritten Notes:
What's the time, Mr. Wolf?
Oh, do fuck off.

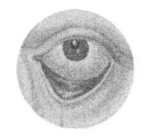

Handwritten Notes:
I wonder what's after steam. Perhaps [remainder of

notebook illegible due to staining].

Random Audio Packet Transcript:
RAP/WI104/Day5/1520-1521
Location: Recreation Area
Present: AK/CF/JP/FN
[00:00:00]
--starts--
Jagrav Panchal: … have you been?
Andrew Keep: Lost. In the woods.
Jagrav Panchal: No shit. You look like you've been dragged backwards through the fucking woods, mate.
Fiona Needles: What's that?
Andrew Keep: My journal.
Jagrav Panchal: No, the other thing.
Andrew Keep: Found it. Just a book.
Cassandra Flint: You should burn it.
Andrew Keep: Why?
Cassandra Flint: [pause] I… I don't know why. I just feel like you should. Like you should burn it.
Andrew Keep: What? Why?
[silence 00:00:14]
Jagrav Panchal: Because it's… an afront to God?
Andrew Keep: What? A what to God?
Jagrav Panchal: [laughs] I don't know. I don't know why I said that. [laughs] Burn it, keep it, I don't give a shit what you do. Just a fucking book, isn't it?
Andrew Keep: Yeah. Just a fucking book.
[silence 00:00:11]
--ends--
[00:01:00]

To: Carl Lyons
Subject: Random Audio Packet Transcript RAP/WI104/Day5/1520-1521
Attached: RAP-WI104/Day5/1520-1521.wav
Morning Sir,
There appear to be no protocols around the whitecoats leaving the Observatory. Could you please advise how to proceed? Also, the almost unconscious reference to an "afront to God"? Does that fall under the 'Religiosity' trigger cited in TO/WHP/WI/EscPro.v12?
Regards,
Ben Hopkirk
Project Administrator
Department of Incidents and Occurrences

To: Ben Hopkirk
Subject: Re: Random Audio Packet Transcript RAP/WI104/Day5/1520-1521
The Observatory is not simply the building. Everything surrounding the structure is also the Observatory. Therefore, Andrew Keep did not leave the Observatory and there is nothing to be

concerned about. However, we may need to get a visual record of this 'book' should things escalate past CompLev 5. For now, just be aware that the book exists.

Regarding your second point, while Religiosity is an Escalation Trigger, it is very unlikely to occur at this early stage. I suspect this may have been a facetious remark, but it is best to treat it with some seriousness. I'll recommend we take the CompLev up to 3, with a view to reducing it should the next 24 hours or so prove uneventful.

Carl Lyons
Senior Project Manager
Department of Incidents and Occurrences

From the DIO Journal of Jagrav Panchal:

What the fuck was that? An afront to God? Where did that even come from? The Kali dreams? They're putting something in the water, they've got to be. Drip. Drip. Drip. Or maybe it's in the air. Every now and then, I'm sure I can smell the temple, the incense. Not those cheap patchouli joss sticks you get from the corner shop. The real stuff: nag champa and agarwood. And then I can smell the food they serve after havan and arthi. I can smell the jeera, dhaniya, haldee, mirch, and the ilaayachee in the rice pudding.

I don't want to sleep. I know I'll dream of Kali. So I tried to read Elmore Leonard. But the words keep moving around until all I can see is God, God, God, God.

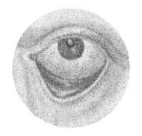

From the DIO Journal of Cassandra Flint:

Why did I tell Andy to burn that awful book-thing? I don't know. I felt so stupid the moment the words were out. Story of my life. I don't even know why it's an 'awful book-thing' and not just a 'book'. It looks like it's made of dirt, dirt and something else. It looks like its filled with things. I don't know what. It looks like it could crawl.

There are more voices now (not just "What's the time, Mr. Wolf?" and I've still no idea who that is) but they don't use any words I can understand. I don't think it's even a foreign language, it's just vowels and consonants and wheezing and hissing. In my head, there's an image of an iron lung, a sentient iron lung. It's filled with frogs and snakes, or things like frogs and snakes but *other*, and it's trying to talk to me, trying to talk to anyone. To everyone.

The silk-across-the-neck feeling has gone. It's been replaced by something worse. A heavy, damp hand resting on my left shoulder. It's there all the time. And the thing I keep seeing out of the periphery of my vision, the fog-trying-to-be-a-person? It has friends now. Six or seven of them, and they're all just as bad at trying to be people. Very bad.

     Oh, and get this, the shitty icing on the shitty cake that has been the last few days: all of my antique VHS tapes have been wiped. They're just static now, just snow and cellophane.

From the DIO Journal of Fiona Needles:

     Blisters on my chest and legs now. I try not to scratch them, but it's hard. When they burst, I'm sure I can hear a little 'ick' sound. The stuff that comes out is like dirty water, but I'm pretty sure it smells of lilacs. When my mum was at the end of her tether with me and my nightmare brother, she'd say, "When I die my corpse will smell of flowers, because I'm a saint to be putting up with all your nonsense!" And me and Patrick would just laugh and carry on causing mayhem. When she died, she didn't smell of flowers. I found her in the bath. Heart attack. Two days she'd been there. The smell was awful. She smelled like the colour she'd turned. At the funeral, I mentioned the whole "my corpse will smell of flowers" thing to Father Atkins and he told me all about The Odour of Sanctity. The sweet odour that emanates from Saints. Even when they're dead. Possibly more so when they're dead. "Osmogenesia" Atkins said was the scientific name for it. I asked him how there could be a scientific word for something with absolutely no basis in science. He looked a bit put-out and then said, "There are massive holes in our understanding, Fiona. Science is full of holes. When they're filled, it won't even be science anymore, it'll be the mind of God." That scared me, scared me a lot, and I don't know why.

I'm no saint, but my leaking blisters smell of lilacs.

The Odour of Sanctity.

Osmogenesia.

What do you make of that, Father Atkins? Am I a hole in science or am I something that might fill said hole?

There's a watercolour on my desk I don't remember painting. It's not very good. Even by my own amateurish standards it's not very good. It is not of a single, tiny, solitary figure. It is not of crowdless me. It looks like a child has painted it. It shows a helicopter crashing into a biplane. If a child had painted it, they would no doubt have added sound effects as the image emerged. A crunching, scraping sound.

I don't know why I painted it, but it felt necessary.

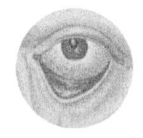

From the private journal of Ben Hopkirk:

I spoke to Sean McMahon again. Lyons is making me nervous. He just doesn't seem to be taking any of this seriously. I know he keeps saying we shouldn't be seeing any unusual activity at this stage, but what if we are?

I asked Sean if he knew anything about the Observatory, how it works, what it's for. He said, "The whole point is not knowing. And that's all I know." What the fuck am I supposed to do with that?

Dad wasn't good today. Not eating, just staring. I know it's horrible to even think about it, but what is the point of even being alive if all you do is stare?

DAY SIX
COMPLEV 3

Random Audio Packet Transcript:
RAP/WI104/Day6/0340-0341
Location: Recreation Area
Present: Unknown
[00:00:00]
--starts--
[silence 00:00:27]
Unknown Female (distorted, almost unintelligible): What's the time, Mr. Wolf?
[silence 00:00:29]
--ends--
[00:01:00]

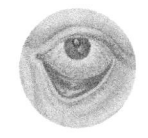

To: Carl Lyons
Subject: Random Audio Packet Transcript RAP/WI104/Day6/0340-0341
Attached: RAP-WI104/Day6/0340-0341.wav
Morning Sir,
Do you think this is cause for concern? It could be Flint or Needles, but it doesn't sound like either of them. Point of fact, it doesn't sound much like a human being.
Regards,
Ben Hopkirk
Project Administrator
Department of Incidents and Occurrences

To: Ben Hopkirk
Subject: Re: Random Audio Packet Transcript RAP/WI104/Day6/0340-0341
Could be a glitch in the surveillance equipment or possibly a corrupted audio file. I'll get someone to look into it.
Carl Lyons
Senior Project Manager
Department of Incidents and Occurrences

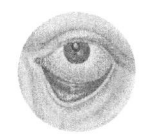

From the DIO journal of Andrew Keep:

I'm staying in my room as much as I can, Sarah. Still doing my tasks (got to watch Mr. Wolf, you know?) but then I'm grabbing one of those Posh Noodles and fucking off back to my quarters. The others are worried about me, which is nice, but I can't risk seeing them. What if I say something? What if somehow they just *know*? Like 'information osmosis' or something? It feels like there's stuff just floating around. Data. Knowing. Percipience.

Thank fuck for Booker T. & the M.G.'s. All the other records, with all those beautiful singers, start skipping the moment I put them on, words jumping out.

God.

Look.

See.

Know.

I put What's Goin' On on the record player and it jumped right to Save the Children and just repeated the same line over and over: "There'll come a time, when the world won't be singin'".

And I haven't told you about the radio, have I? Jesus. I went up there, to the second floor. I wasn't sure what I was planning to do. Was I going to radio for help? Maybe. But that would have been insane, wouldn't it? I mean, that would be like putting Mr. Wolf on a helicopter and sending him to the UK, into the world. He's got a disease, Mr. Wolf. Like rabies but it can turn the human race into stains and steam.

Anyway, it didn't matter what I was planning to do or what I wasn't planning to do because the radio's a joke. It's hollow. It's just a box. There's nothing in it. There aren't even wires and circuit boards and valves pretending to be useful. It's a fucking prop. Like those computers and TVs you get in Ikea. It's a fucking Ikea radio! I lifted the whole thing up with two hands and held it over my head. It weighed nothing. And then I put it down, went back to my room and laughed until I cried.

From the DIO journal of Cassandra Flint:

They haven't been wiped. My video tapes. It's not static. I don't know why I thought it was. It's too… milky. And there's something swimming around in that milkiness. At first, I thought it was people, or things trying very hard and failing very badly to look like people. But then it was James Stewart as John Ferguson, Bogart as Sam Spade, Ray Milland as Don Birnam, and Orson Wells and Janet Leigh as Hank Quinlan and Susie Vargas. But only for a few seconds and then they came together into one thing. One thing with too many arms. Like one of those Hindu gods, but warped and milky and a mess.

  Christ, I am so fucking tired. Must be run down. Some kind of rash on my arms, almost like little pinhead blisters. Impetigo?

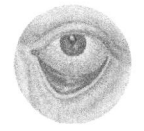

From the DIO journal of Jagrav Panchal.

Greetings to the triumphant one, the propitious one, Kālī, who is outside time and space, who is a manifestation of Shakti, who wears a garland of skulls around her neck, and is also called Durgā, the merciful mother of the earth, who is the murderer of Madhu and Kaiṭabha the demons who crawled from the ear of Vishnu when he slept his Yoga Nidra sleep.

Kitne baje hain, Shreemaan Bhediya?

What the fuck? Why am I writing this shit.

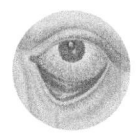

From the DIO journal of Fiona Needles:

I can feel them, overlapping me. Occupying the same space as me. Not people, though. Not really. Maybe they were people once, but not anymore. I can't see them. Not really. Maybe sometimes from the corner of my eye and just for a moment. I can smell them, though. Lilacs. Like the stuff that's leaking from my blisters. I don't even have to burst them now. They just pop all on their own.

I need to speak to the others. It can't be just me going through this, can it? But every time I'm about to bring it up, my mouth dries out and I don't have the words.

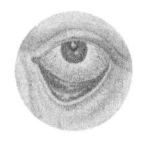

Random Audio Packet Transcript:

RAP/WI104/Day6/1730-1731
Location: Recreation Area
Present: AK/CF/JP/FN
[00:00:00]
--starts--
Andrew Keep: ... go first, then. Favourite song, Inner City Blues by Marvin Gaye. Favourite Film, that's a tough one, but I'd probably have to go with Taxi Driver... no, Serpico. Love that one. Favourite book, Devil in a Blue Dress by Walter Mosley. Who's next?
Cassandra Flint: I'll go. Song would be Get Lucky by Daft Punk. Film would be Hot Tub Time Machine. Book... Probably The Buddha of Suburbia by Hanif Kureishi?
Jagrav Panchal: Hot Tub Time Machine?
Cassandra Flint: Yeah. John Cusack is my happy place.
Jagrav Panchal: He must have been in something better than Hot Tub Time Machine.
Cassandra Flint: I would contend that nobody has been in anything better than Hot Tub Time Machine, but it is getting late and I'm very tired.
[laughter]
Cassandra Flint: What about you Jag?
Jagrav Panchal: Okay. I'll start with the film. That's going to have to be Hot Tub Time Machine...
[laughter: 00:00:11]
--ends--
[00:01:00]

To: Carl Lyons
Subject: Random Audio Packet Transcript RAP/WI104/Day6/1730-1731
Attached: RAP-WI104/Day6/1730-1731.wav

Evening Sir,

Not sure if you're likely to get this until the morning. I hope you're still up and logged on.

That last audio packet, I knew there was something wrong with it, but I couldn't put my finger on what it was. It sounded like it was from the first day. Just the way they were talking, like they were introducing themselves. I was so busy listening to the tone, I missed the obvious. Flint says it's getting late and she's very tired, but the RAP is time-stamped five-thirty in the evening.

Sir, what if someone's tampering with the feeds?

Regards,

Ben Hopkirk
Project Administrator
Department of Incidents and Occurrences

DAY SEVEN
COMPLEV 3

To: Ben Hopkirk
Subject: Re: Random Audio Packet Transcript RAP/WI104/Day6/1730-1731

Just got your email now. You should have called. Contact Beverley Hobbes at AV-Surv. Request an immediate Live Audio Feed. No more than three minutes. Tell her to redact all non-human vocalisations. That is critical. If she asks for an approval code, quote CL-SPM-18-90-19-37-46. She's unlikely to ask for any further detail, but if she does, refer her to me. Tell her nothing else. Nothing else. I want a status report no more than one hour from now.

Carl Lyons
Senior Project Manager
Department of Incidents and Occurrences

Live Audio Feed Transcript LAF/WI104/Day7/0818-0821
Location: Recreation Area
Present: CF/JP/FN
[00:00:00]
--starts--
Fiona Needles: ...be the only one who's feeling this fucked-up.
Jagrav Panchal: I'm feeling okay. I think. I mean, I've been thinking a lot about things I've never really

given much thought to before, religious stuff, Hindu stuff, but I don't know, it's... I think it's fine. I feel okay. I think.
Fiona Needles: Religious stuff. Yeah. Me too. Saints. Osmogenesia. The Odour of Sanctity. Fucking blisters all over the place. Lilacs. They smell of lilacs. The stuff in them does.
Jagrav Panchal: Lilacs?
Cassandra Flint: Seeing things. Like steam that's trying to be people. Out of the corner of my eye.
Fiona Needles: Yes! That! Fuck.
Cassandra Flint: I should be used to it. I've been seeing things, hearing things, receiving things, since I was a little kid. I should be used to this shit. But I'm not. This is different. It's not people. It's... I don't know... I don't know what it is. Something. There's a fucking... what? A fucking... bigness to it. A bigness.
Jagrav Panchal: What do you mean, since you were a kid?
Cassandra Flint: What?
Jagrav Panchal: What do you mean you've been seeing and hearing stuff since you were a kid?
Cassandra Flint: Just what I said. I'm sensitive. Mostly, I like it. But sometimes it gets a bit much. When it does, I just smoke a little weed, get a little high, and it goes away. But I don't have any weed. And it won't go away. I don't think there's enough weed in the world to get rid of this thing.
Fiona Needles: It's like you said on day one, Cassie, maybe we're the experiment. There must be

something in the water or in the food or in the air. Or maybe they're transmitting subliminal messages, like ultrasound or something, to get us thinking about stuff, putting ideas in our heads.

Cassandra Flint: Yeah. Yeah. It's like being injected with thoughts.

Fiona Needles: It's like poisoning.

Jagrav Panchal: Poisoning.

Fiona Needles: And what about Andy? He just stays in his room. When he's not out on the observation deck. What was that book he brought back? Where'd he get that?

Cassandra Flint: I didn't like it. That book thing.

Jagrav Panchal: Yeah.

Fiona Needles: I don't like any of this. We should use that radio upstairs. We should call them, whoever's doing this, tell them to stop, tell them we want to come home now and we've had enough.

Jagrav Panchal: Will we still get paid? I don't want Kali to break my fucking legs.

Fiona Needles: What? Don't want Kali to break your legs?

Jagrav Panchal: [laughs] Not Kali. Khalid. Aziz Khalid. That fucking cunt.

[redacted]

Cassandra Flint: Did you hear that? Was that in my head?

Fiona Needles: I... I heard it. Jesus. What was that?

[redacted]

Cassandra Flint: ...fuck is that?

[redacted 00:00:18]

Jagrav Panchal: Ah. Fuck. Ah. Don't want to hear that. Don't want to.
[redacted 00:00:28]
Fiona Needles: That word… it's… too big. That word is too big.
[redacted]
Jagrav Panchal: Samay kya hua hai, Shreemaan Bhediya? [Hindi. Translation: What's the time, Mr. Wolf?]
--ends--
[00:03:00]

DIO Telephone Transcript:
DIOTT/WI104/Day7/0913
Between Carl Lyons, Senior Project Manager, and Ben Hopkirk, Project Administrator.
--starts--
Carl Lyons: What the fuck, Hopkirk? What the fuck?
Ben Hopkirk: Sir, I've been trying to –
Carl Lyons: How did we end up with a fucking… a… fucking psychic on the… fuck. An esper? Fuck.
Ben Hopkirk: Esper? I don't… uh. Esper?
Carl Lyons: Flint. The Flint woman. A fucking esper. This whole thing's supposed to be a slow burn. Steady as she goes. Steady as she fucking goes, Hopkirk. An esper, a fucking phrenic… that's like pouring petrol on the whole thing. Jesus. A fucking

phrenic!

Ben Hopkirk: I don't know what that is, sir. I don't uh. Uh psychics aren't… you know. Are they?

Carl Lyons: They are. Everything is. Everything you think isn't fucking is. Out there somewhere. How the fuck? [pause] Who pre-selected her?

Ben Hopkirk: I don't… hang on… I'll check.

[background noise 00:00:19]

Carl Lyons: Lyons? Speed it up. Speed. It. Up.

Ben Hopkirk: I'm just…

[background noise]

Ben Hopkirk: Here it… just one… uh… Blackford, sir. It was Gareth Blackford, sir.

Carl Lyons: [pause] The same… the same Blackford who was on chauffeur duty for WI104?

Ben Hopkirk: Well… I… Yes, I assume it's the same one.

Carl Lyons: That isn't… That's a protocol breach. Only one task. No overlaps. Why didn't you tell me?

Ben Hopkirk: Sir, I didn't know. Everything I know is on a handful of… of fucking laminated recipe cards, sir. Just fucking bullet points and half of them don't make sense. I was told that was the point. That not knowing is the point… isn't it?

[background noise]

Ben Hopkirk: Sir?

Carl Lyons: Take the day off. Don't speak to anybody about this. Anybody. Do you understand?

Ben Hopkirk: No sir. I… don't understand. I don't understand any of this shit.

Carl Lyons: That's good. That's good.

Ben Hopkirk: What... what's going to happen now? To the... the whitecoats? Has this happened before? What happens, you know, next? To them.
Carl Lyons: Take the day off. Don't worry about it. I'll speak to you tomorrow. Or the day after. I'll speak to you when I speak to you.
Ben Hopkirk: But isn't there
--ends--

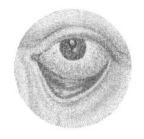

To: Beverley Hobbes
Subject: LVF Request for WI104
Hi Bev,
Hope you're doing well. Sorry to hear about your mum and glad she's on the mend now. Hope you and Sarah are keeping okay. Send her my regards. Thanks for sorting the Live Audio Feed for Ben. Much appreciated. As you've no doubt guessed there have been a few irregularities at The Observatory. Minor stuff. Nothing to worry about. I don't want to start pointing fingers, but Mr Hopkirk might not have been the best recruitment decision I've made! Never mind, we all make mistakes! Could you possibly send me a Live Video Feed, please? Just a two-minute segment. Want to make sure everything's tickety-boo. Sure it is, but just to be on the safe side. My authorisation code is CL-SPM-18-90-19-37-46.
Carl Lyons

Senior Project Manager
Department of Incidents and Occurrences

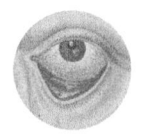

To: Carl Lyons
Subject: Re: LVF Request for WI104
Attached: LVF-WI104/Day7/recroom/0943-0945.mp4

Hi Carl,

Mum's a lot better now, thanks. It was touch and go for a while, though, and she gave us quite a scare. I'll tell Sarah you said hi. No problem with the LVF. I can only give you one camera, though (protocol!), so I've gone with the rec area, camera three. And, obviously, I can't give you audio *and* video. We'd need Director Kendall's approval for that. So, it's going to be a silent movie, I'm afraid. Hope that's okay.

Take care. Speak to you soon hopefully.

Beverley Hobbes
Senior AV Technician
Department of Incidents and Occurrences

Transcript of LVF-WI104/Day7/recroom/9043-0945.mp4:

THE OBSERVATORY – RECREATION AREA – CAMERA 3

CASSANDRA FLINT and FIONA NEEDLES are sat on the sofa.

JAGRAV PANCHAL is sat opposite them on the coffee table.

ANDREW KEEP is standing to one side. He is carrying a thick book. It is not an official DIO journal.

They are all talking in an animated fashion. It is difficult to make out individual expressions, but body language suggests an argument or, at the very least, a heated discussion.

[There appears to be a glitch at this point. The image becomes milky for approximately eight seconds, as if an opalescent film has formed on the camera's lens. During this time, six or seven shapes, possibly humanoid in design, can be seen moving toward the recreation area. At the five-second mark, the shapes appear to coalesce into a single 'figure' with multiple 'limbs'. The 'figure' turns on the spot, increasing in speed until it becomes tornado-like. Then the glitch abruptly resolves itself.]

A man walks into frame from the direction of the main staircase. He is wearing a DIO uniform. He is talking to the whitecoats, his hands raised in a placatory fashion.

As he nears the camera, it becomes apparent that the man is GARETH BLACKFORD.

Blackford, one hand still raised in a calming gesture, points back to the stairs.

[Another glitch. The screen turns black, from the centre out. The blackness is not absolute. There is a sense of looking down into deep, dark waters. There is something moving through those waters, something vast that looks like a violent, penetrating collision of squid and octopus and lobster and Portuguese man o' war. It convulses, sending constellations of gleaming bubbles up toward the viewer. Then the glitch resolves itself.]

Keep, Flint, Panchal, Needles and Blackford are gone.

DIO Telephone Transcript:
DIOTT/WI104/Day7/1017
Between Project Director Kendal and Carl Lyons, Senior Project Manager.
--starts--
Project Director Kendall: [redacted]
Carl Lyons: Yes, sir.
Project Director Kendall: [redacted]
Carl Lyons: No… well… I didn't… No. No, sir.
Project Director Kendall: [redacted]
Carl Lyons: An empath, sir. A phrenic.
Project Director Kendall: [redacted]
Carl Lyons: Blackford, sir. Initially. Then Hopkirk. Ben Hopkirk.
Project Director Kendall: [redacted]

Carl Lyons: Yes. Blackford.
Project Director Kendall: [redacted]
Carl Lyons: No. Not for at least 24 hours, sir.
Project Director Kendall: [redacted]
Carl Lyons: Helicopter, sir.
Project Director Kendall: [redacted]
Carl Lyons: Yes.
Project Director Kendall: [redacted]
Carl Lyons: We don't know.
Project Director Kendall: [redacted]
Carl Lyons: We don't know that either, sir, I'm afraid.
Project Director Kendall: [redacted]
Carl Lyons: No. Of course not, sir, of course not.
Project Director Kendall: [redacted]
Carl Lyons: Yes.
Project Director Kendall: [redacted]
Carl Lyons: We couldn't have—
Project Director Kendall: [redacted]
Carl Lyons: No. No, sir.
Project Director Kendall: [redacted]
Carl Lyons: Yes, sir. I will.
Project Director Kendall: [redacted]
Carl Lyons: Everything we can. We have something ready to go to the media with already, sir.
Project Director Kendall: [redacted]
Carl Lyons: Yes, sir.
--ends—

DAY EIGHT
COMPLEV 9

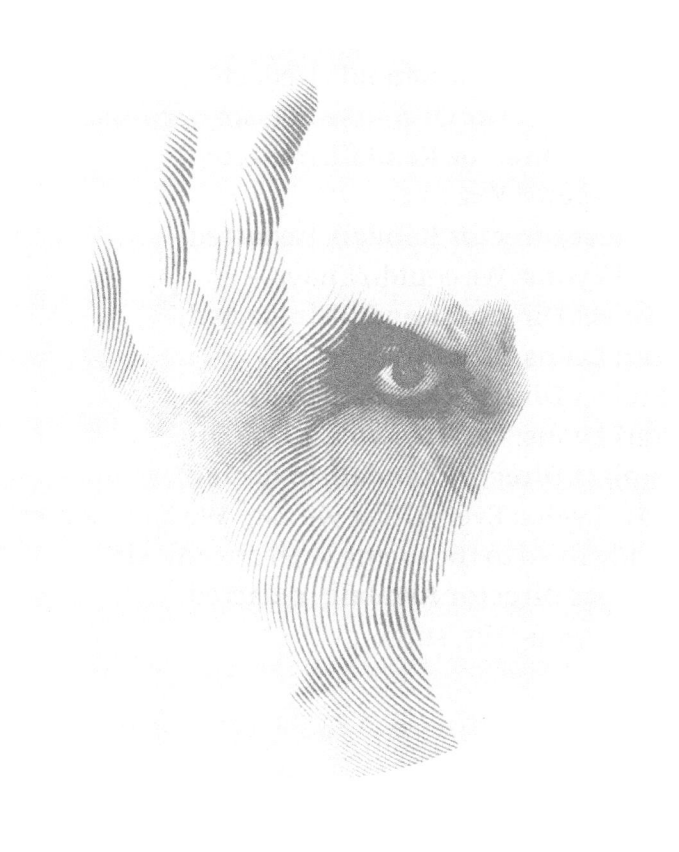

From the front page of The Daily Mail (2024, September 2nd):

Terrorist Cell Members Identified
The Home Office have released details of the terrorist cell disrupted just days from carrying out an attack that could have seen hundreds dead and potentially thousands injured at Manchester's Piccadilly Station.

A significant quantity of explosives was found at a house in the Fallowfield district of the city, as well as a detailed map of Piccadilly Station and the surrounding area. The property is now believed to have belonged to Andrew Keep (top left), potentially the terrorist cell's principal. The other members have been identified as Jagrav Panchal (top right), Fiona Needles (bottom right) and Cassandra Flint (bottom left). Little is known about these individuals at this stage, including to which terrorist organisation they might be affiliated, but we've been told that full details will be released before the end of the day.

The authorities are certain the group are somewhere in the UK, likely separated, but they have as of yet given no indication of where. A Home Office official told us "They must be considered highly dangerous. Report any sightings or suspected sightings to the police immediately. Do not approach these people under any circumstances."

DAY TWENTY-THREE
COMPLEV 12

DIO Telephone Transcript:
DIOTT/WI104/Day23/0837
Between Project Director Kendal and Carl Lyons, Senior Project Manager.
--starts--
Project Director Kendall: [redacted]
Carl Lyons: We don't know, sir,
Project Director Kendall: [redacted]
Carl Lyons: Uploaded this morning, sir. We don't have a location yet.
Project Director Kendall: [redacted]
Carl Lyons: The original was taken down immediately, sir, within minutes. But dupes have already started to appear. We're swatting them as and when.
Project Director Kendall: [redacted]
Carl Lyons: No. No, sir. I really have no fucking idea.

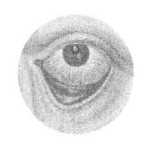

YouTube Video
Uploaded by user Percipience37451270.
43,412 views • Sep 17, 2024

TITLE CARD: PERCIPIENCE

BACKGROUND MUSIC: Philly Dog by the Mar-Keys

FADE IN:

INT. HOTEL ROOM – DAY

GARETH BLACKFORD is sitting in a cheap aluminium and vinyl chair. On the wall behind him is a mirror. In the mirror we can see there is a table in front of him. On the table, mounted on a miniature tripod, is the mobile phone that is recording this video. Between the phone and Blackford is a sort of book. It looks like it has been handmade. It also looks like it has been dug up out of a peat bog. Blackford is wearing a green Star Wars t-shirt. His arms, neck and face are covered in what appear to be blisters. He looks both exhausted and euphoric.

BLACKFORD

> So, who's ready for a whole new world? Huh? Everybody, surely. I mean, this shitshow, this absolute fucking clown toilet cannot be allowed to continue. Right? Right. Time for a shift. A paradigm shift. Time for a new god.
>
> We call it The Obscurity. But that's not its name. We don't know what its name is and might not even be able to pronounce it when we find out, but that's what we call it for now. The Obscurity.
>
> Think of it as a placeholder. Lorem ipsum.

My friend Jagrav Panchal – not a terrorist, by the way. Jesus, those DIO pricks – thought for a while that it might be Kali. The Kali of 'terrible countenance, armed with a sword and noose'. But he was wrong. He realised that before he died, before he became steam.

They're all steam now. Cassie, Fiona and Andy. They did not go quietly or peacefully or painlessly but they did go knowingly. Some people take longer to sublime than others. Cynicism and stupidity seem to slow down the process, which makes sense. They're both the enemy of knowing, of percipience. But grief? Wow. Grief really slows it down. I don't know why. Maybe because grief is the suspension of all possibility. When you're grieving, I mean really fucking grieving, snot and ashes, nothing seems possible. It's the end of everything. Isn't it? There's nothing *to* understand.

Andy was the last to go. And I've hung on longer than anyone. Me and Andy are alike. Grievers. The slow-motion bullet of grief hit me in the heart two years ago and it's been burrowing its way through all that dead tissue like a lead maggot ever since. Andy lost his Sarah. And I lost my David. I miss my husband. I really fucking miss him.

Fuck.

Blackford begins to cry, but only for ten, fifteen seconds. He sniffs hard and brings himself under control.

> Christ. Tears and weeping sores do not mix. That is a very effective recipe for some serious stinging. Feels like I've got a face full of wasps.
>
> I'm going to be honest with you, I don't know what's going to happen next. I don't know what this new world, this new paradigm, will look like. Paradigm might even be the wrong word. It might be the end of paradigms, the end of states, of fixedness. But it might be the death of death. The reversing of time's arrow. Or the shattering of time's arrow. The return of husbands and wives like they were never gone and never could ever have been gone. It might be the evaporation of hatred and sadness. Like, 'What were all those horrible feelings we had? I don't know. They just upped and went. They seem so silly now.' It might be a glorious, terrifying, eternal fucking nightmare. But it has to be better than this. Has to be.

Look around you. Pick up a newspaper. Flick through the too-many channels of your too-big TV. Doomscroll through your social media toxin of choice. And tell me the world isn't irredeemably fucked, an unhealing wound infected with a stupidity and selfishness so intense it reaches for suicide with all the blind and thoughtless glee of a toddler snatching at shiny objects.

He scratches his forearms vigorously.

Jesus but these things fucking itch.

He stops scratching and sniffs his fingers.

Lilacs.

He leans closer to the phone. We can't see the mirror anymore, just his face.

Here it is in a nutshell.

There's this thing. A god. It's waiting just outside our reality. Our paradigm. Waiting. It's been there a long time, perhaps all the time. To bring it, all we need to do is understand it. We must know The Obscurity. It mustn't remain obscure. To understand it is to admit it. In both senses of the word. To acknowledge or accept as valid and to allow someone, something, to gain access. The sentence that begins 'The Obscurity is' must be completed.

I have no idea how it should be completed. That's up to you. But here's a few 'starters for ten'.

The Obscurity is a god.

The Obscurity is God.

The Obscurity is a massive extra-dimensional energy field that got drawn inside a black hole eight billion years ago.

The Obscurity is the point at which all ideas collapse.

The Obscurity is the creation myth the Gods look to when they wonder who made them.

The Obscurity is a flavour that you feel with your eyes.

The Obscurity is the answer to the question 'Why are there any anythings?'

The Obscurity is the bowl of soup inside the crouton.

The Obscurity is spacetime foam dripping from the jaws of a rabid but well-meaning Cerberus.

The Obscurity is The Obscurity.

The Obscurity is my husband.

The Obscurity is me.

The Obscurity is you.

Blackford leans toward the phone, smiling.

The Obscurity is you.

He stiffens. His smile falters then drops. His left eye looks wrong. Bulgy, askew, a rapidly developing strabismus. His teeth clench and his lips draw back. Slowly, his left eye emerges from its socket.

The... Obscurity... is you.

The eye slithers down his cheek, trailing something like wet, black mould. The mould steams. From the dark of the socket a pale digit, not quite a finger, emerges. It makes a single, shaky circular motion, as if it is trying to draw a letter 'o' or a zero in the air.

The image begins to shake and fragment. White

fibres twitch across the screen. Blackford, his mouth painfully wide, starts to scream.

CUT TO BLACK

DAY THIRTY-SEVEN
COMPLEV 13

Graffiti on the sandstone wall above the Penny Lane street sign, Liverpool: The Obscurity is The Walrus.

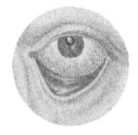

Graffiti on the ground before William Blake's memorial stone, Bunhill Fields, London: The Obscurity is Urthona,

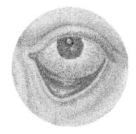

Graffiti on the wall of Federico Fellini's home, Parioli, Rome: l'oscurità è otto e mezzo.

Graffiti on the wall of 1126 Francisco Street, Berkeley, California: The Obscurity is Ubik.

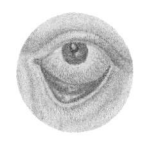

Graffiti on the wall of 1010 Montgomery Street, North Beach, San Francisco: The Obscurity is

Rockland.

Graffiti on the door of the Full Gospel Tabernacle Church, Memphis, Tennessee: The Obscurity is so tired of being alone.

From the private journal of Ben Hopkirk:

I'm not going to write about it. I'm not even going to fucking think about it.

DIO motherfuckers. Department of Idiots and… something beginning with 'o' that means dickheads.

Not my problem anymore. Not going to think about it.

Motherfuckers.

Terrorists my arse. My fucking arse. What the fuck was all that about?

Jesus.

And that video. What the fuck? Made no sense. But there were triggers all over it. Religion. Blisters. The Obscurity? What is that? Is that what they were observing at the Observatory?

Not my problem. None of it matters.

Motherfuckers.

All that 'the Obscurity is' graffiti, I get. Millions of people have seen that video now. But what about all those people in white coats? Just walking the streets, sitting on the bus, propping up lampposts, wandering around in the background of *every single* piece of news footage. Who the fuck are they? And how do they know? How do they know about the white coats? About the whitecoats? There was nothing about that on Blackford's video, nothing in the newspapers or on the telly. How do they know? And what do they mean, the white coats? It's like everyone knows what's going on but me.

Anyway. Forget all that. Forget the mass disappearances. Forget the 'steam people' sightings. It's one step down from Big Foot and the Yeti. It's the Loch Ness fucking Monster. Fuck all that shit. I don't want to know. I feel safer not knowing. Not thinking about it. Not talking about it. Not writing about it.

My dad, that's what I'm going to write about. He's like a new man. I spoke to Doctor Matthewman this afternoon and he can't explain it. Said he was reluctant to use the word 'miracle' but he couldn't think of another word that would more accurately capture my dad's transformation. And it is a transformation. I saw him a few days ago and there was no change. He was staring at the wall or at his hands like there was something important there he might be able to understand or unlock if he just stared hard enough. He called me Brian and asked me if I'd stolen his toothbrush. All the usual shit. And it broke my heart more than usual because of all the DIO bullshit, all the confusion and anger it had sown in my head. That's why I skipped a few days. Normally I see him every day. But I couldn't face it. Just fucking couldn't. But today… a new man. Standing, walking, talking. Not just weird, random outbursts of words and phrases, but actual small talk, conversation. He was smiling, too. Smiling and laughing. It was lovely. He looked younger. The lines around his eyes were a little less deep, a little less like scars. There were threads of black in his grey hair.

    Just one little lapse, just as I was leaving.
    He said, "What's the time, Mr. Wolf?"
    I said, "What?"
    He said, "Nothing."

ABOUT THE AUTHOR

Michael Sellars

Michael Sellars was forced to begin writing stories as a child when Liverpool's libraries struggled to satisfy his appetite for horror, fantasy and science fiction.

He has published the novel, Hyenas (from Northodox Press); the novella, Things Not Made; the short-story collection, Heartfelt Horrors; and the standalone short story The Meat Just Falls From the Bone (all proceeds to Medical Aid for Palestinians).

He has contributed stories to All Hallows, Murky Depths, Nocturne, Fusing Horizons, Morpheus Tales, the Best Tales of the Apocalypse anthology from Permuted Press and the From the Trenches anthology from Carnifex Press.

He is currently working on a new horror novel, Choking Hazards, and a sequel to Hyenas with the working title of Tygers.

He is represented by the Liverpool Literary Agency

(www.liverpool-literary.agency).

He can be found on Twitter/X as @horrorpaperback.

Printed in Great Britain
by Amazon